ALL OVER AMERICA,
THE TIMES, THEY WERE A-CHANGING.

BUT THE NEWS HADN'T REACHED
A GOOD OL' SMALL TOWN IN MISSISSIPPI.

If you were white, you were right.

If you were black, you stood back.

And if you tried to change the way things were,
you were as good as dead in a place where
flaming crosses lit the blood-dark summer of
1964 with the fire of hate. . . .

MISSISSIPPI BURNING

Mississippi Burning

a novel by Joel Norst

based on a screenplay written by
Chris Gerolmo

A SIGNET BOOK

NEW AMERICAN LIBRARY

THIS FILM WAS INSPIRED BY ACTUAL EVENTS
WHICH TOOK PLACE IN THE SOUTH DURING THE 1960'S.
THE CHARACTERS, HOWEVER, ARE FICTITIOUS
AND DO NOT DEPICT REAL PEOPLE EITHER LIVING OR DEAD.

PUBLISHER'S NOTE

This book is a work of fiction. Names, characters, places, and incidents either are the product of the author's imagination or are used fictitiously, and any resemblance to actual persons, living or dead, events, or locales is entirely coincidental.

SIGNET TRADEMARK REG. U.S. PAT. OFF. AND FOREIGN COUNTRIES
REGISTERED TRADEMARK—MARCA REGISTRADA
HECHO EN CHICAGO, U.S.A.

SIGNET, SIGNET CLASSIC, MENTOR, ONYX, PLUME, MERIDIAN
and NAL BOOKS are published by NAL PENGUIN INC.,
1633 Broadway, New York, New York 10019

First Printing, December, 1988

  2 3 4 5 6 7 8 9

PRINTED IN THE UNITED STATES OF AMERICA

1

"Who the hell . . . ?"

Clutching the steering wheel at ten and two o'clock, the driver stared over his white knuckles and out the windshield. A kind of tunnel was being formed in the thick loblolly pines by the headlamps of his Country Squire station wagon. Some of this light was spilling back over the Ford's dusty hood, catching the damp, pale face of the young man sharing the front seat with him.

The driver glanced at the rearview mirror. "What are they doing to us?"

The Negro youth in the backseat didn't respond, although the driver could make out the silhouette of his head outlined against the reddish glow of the Ford's tail lamps.

This glow was reflecting off the chrome grill of the passenger car that was following them.

The car was running without lights—and no more than a foot off the station wagon's rear bumper. Somewhere in the last wooded mile, it had fallen behind them.

The driver was going slow enough to hear crickets out his side window. And beyond the reach of his headlamps, fireflies were winking on and off.

Fireflies had always seemed magical to him: he remembered the first fireflies of the New Jersey evening sparking out in his parents' backyard.

He realized that his right hand had gravitated to his wispy goatee and was kneading it. Would it ever fill in enough to be considered a proper beard?

"What do we do now?" the youth beside him asked.

"I don't know." The driver raised his voice a little for the benefit of their Negro friend in the backseat. "Any ideas?"

But he said nothing. Over these past weeks they had spent together—manning a rickety cardboard table cluttered with voter registration forms and instructions, sleeping in moldy church basements —he had invariably reacted to any hint of danger with silence. It seemed his weapon of last resort.

The driver asked himself if he too had a weapon of last resort. Did a person who believed in nonviolence have one?

On a hunch he slowed even more and, extending his thin arm out the open window, waved for the car to go around. "Enough already," he whispered.

But the offer was refused. The driver thought he could hear laughter from behind.

"Christ." Something white and shiny on the pavement caught his eye. It stank of death in passing. "What was the hell was that?"

"Canebreak rattler," the Negro youth said.

It had been belly-up, repeatedly flattened by tires.

The driver found it difficult to believe that there was ever enough traffic out here to catch a rattlesnake napping. Maybe it had been squashed by one of the logging trucks that, over the years, had ground the asphalt down to washboards on the curves.

"Let's get back to some lights," the youth beside him said in a low voice. He was from New York city—the upper West Side—and used to lots of lights. His first observation about Mississippi had been how dark it turned as soon as the sun was gone.

"Any major towns this way?" the driver asked the Negro youth.

"No big towns this way for miles and miles. Just woods. Some cypress swamp farther southwest. But no lights."

Something in these words raised the hair on the back of the driver's neck—the resignation in them, perhaps.

His father's 1959 Country Squire had five years of hard commuter miles on its V8 engine, which dieseled for at least a full minute after the key was switched off. The front end was in dire need of alignment: twice on the trip down, he had been pulled over by Southern state troopers on the groundless suspicion that he was drunk. And both rear tires were as smooth as bowling balls.

But he had made up his mind. "Let's get the hell out of here."

"You sure?"

He briefly met his front passenger's uncertain gaze. "Yeah." He jammed the automatic shift down into low gear and accelerated until the pedal was pressing against the worn carpet of the floor mat.

He could feel the Negro youth lean forward and drape his forearms across the top of the front seat. His breaths were hot and quick. "Be watching the curves. Rough road."

"Okay," the driver said quietly.

The toe of his tennis sneaker found the button on the firewall, and he clicked on the high beams. They danced and skittered up in the whiskery foliage of the pines. The trunks made whooshing sounds as they rushed past and receded into the darkness.

He had imagined that the speed would make him feel braver. But the shuddering of the Ford over the corrugated road became his own. And his hands had begun to ache from grasping the wheel too tightly. He had also hoped that the in-rushing wind would refresh him, but it was as stifling as the night itself.

The red speedometer needle was vibrating between seventy-five and eighty. His father had warned him not to overtax the tired engine.

The Negro youth gripped his shoulder. "Be watching this curve now. This ain't no turnpike."

"I will . . . I will."

Yet the driver took the sharp bend with too much speed. The sound of gravel rattling in the wheel wells on his side told him that he'd arced out onto the far shoulder.

Then he overcorrected, and the Country Squire lurched wildly from berm to berm before he could steady it again.

One or both of the passengers had shouted "Jesus!" in this split second the station wagon was out of control—he wasn't sure. Maybe he had cried out, too.

At last, on a fairly straight section over some grassy swampland, he allowed himself a glance at the rearview mirror.

"Son of bitch," he said, his voice breaking.

The passenger car, a two-tone sedan he now saw, was still giving chase.

For all his risky antics, the driver had gained less than fifty feet on it. And even more discouraging, he could now discern the shapes of two other vehicles following the first: a dark-colored older model pickup truck and a white Galaxie.

They too were speeding without lights.

Suddenly his mirror filled with a blaze of high beams. Through this dazzle he barely picked out the red light rotating on the roof of the sedan.

"Shit! Another cop!" His tennis sneaker backed off the pedal, and the Ford rumbled to a stop on a turnout just before the road began winding into the pines again. "What are these jokers playing at?"

"Oh, they ain't playing," the Negro youth said as soon as the engine had died.

The driver took his hands off the steering wheel, and folded them in his lap to keep them from shaking. They were sweaty but unnaturally cool. Taking a few breaths so his voice wouldn't quaver, he said, "Sit tight, guys. Don't say anything—"

"I want to get out," the youth beside him interrupted, his fist wrapped around the door latch. "I need to stand up."

"No," the driver said.

"Please."

"Stay where you are. And let me do the talking. We'll be okay. Relax."

The three of them fell silent, facing forward but listening hard for any sound from behind.

The lockstep singing of the crickets made the driver grind his teeth. Never had he heard such shrill, insistent crickets.

After several long moments he heard heavy footfalls approach over the gravel. More than one man was closing on the Ford.

He squeezed his eyes shut for a second, struggling to ease the fear off his face. Then he peered through the windshield again. It needed washing, he thought idly.

He had left his headlamps on, and bugs were swirling in the beams as if drunk on the light. Thousands of bugs. And he'd always thought that a New Jersey summer was lousy with bugs.

Several flashlights came on at once. One was so close he was sure he could feel the warmth of the bulb on his cheek.

"Y'all think you can drive any goddamn speed you want around here?"

"You had us scared to death, man."

"Don't you call me 'man,' Jew-boy."

They knew who he was. As he had dimly suspected from the moment he'd realized he was being followed, this had been arranged. Yet he continued to stare forward, expressionless.

The fear had completely opened his nostrils to the humid night, and he could now smell the pines keenly. He concentrated on this pleasant odor in an effort to quell the anger that was waiting to shoot out of his mouth. He had had quite a mouth as a school kid, and controlling it had not been easy. "Very well, sir. What should I call you?" He had been trained to sound this way: civil but not obsequious.

From the other side of the station wagon came a second voice: "You don't call us nothing, nigger-lover Jew-boy. You just listen."

"Hah," yet another man said, his words punctuated by the slosh of liquid in a bottle being upturned, "you just listen now."

He found it difficult to keep track of everything that was going on around the station wagon. Someone was talking to the Negro youth: "What you saying there, boy?"

"Fine, sir."

Then a face drew close to the driver's, and the man started making exaggerated sniffing noises like a hound in a cartoon.

"You even starting to smell like a nigger, you know that?"

A voice on the far side of the Ford then suggested that niggers smelled for all the world like sheep.

"Goats," another man argued, and the driver felt as if he were getting dizzy. And then it seemed as if he were growing tiny, shrinking into the seat.

The youth beside him had begun to hyperventilate.

"Take it easy," he told him. "We'll be all right."

"Sure you will," the man at his window said jocularly, and laughter followed from all around. But it seemed overly nervous.

Then the laughter faded, and the cricket songs welled into prominence once again.

These crickets must be as big as mice, he thought.

The abrupt quiet in the men made him turn into the flashlight beam. "Why are we being detained again?" he asked evenly.

"He just seen your face," someone behind the station wagon warned. "That ain't good."

"That ain't nothing."

"You don't want him seeing your face, do you?"

After a moment the man at the window said with a faraway hollowness to his voice: "It don't make no difference."

Then the driver felt something metallic tap against his skull a few inches behind his left ear.

He craned far enough to see that it was a revolver. Then he froze. He tried to think of something to say, but nothing came into his mind except a list-less, almost drowsy certainty that this had deterio-rated too swiftly for talk to do any good. Nothing was going to do any good ever again.

"Oh Jesus," the youth beside him moaned.

The driver heard nothing to tell him that the trigger had been pulled, that the hammer had snicked back and then fallen forward. But sud-denly the inside of his head was aswarm with fireflies. He had never seen so many fireflies.

His elbow hanging out the rolled-down passen-ger window of the black Dodge Polara, Special Agent Rupert Anderson watched the Delta coun-try roll past under an already oppressive mid-morning sun. Mississippi's Delta region wasn't much like neighboring Louisiana's—a triangle of heaped-up silt at the mouth of the great muddy flow; it was just the name everybody had settled on for the ancient floodplain of the Yazoo and Missis-sippi rivers. But regardless of whether or not the name fit, the same sort of cotton fields sloped away to steamy-looking creeks—except now the land was planted in as much soybeans and milo as cotton. King Cotton didn't even qualify as a duke nowadays. Not that Anderson would ever shed a tear over it: sometimes in his sleep he still found himself picking the stuff from "can to can't," drag-ging a duck sack along the furrow behind him.

He started whistling between his teeth, search-ing for a tune that might fit the sloppily mimeo-graphed lyrics he was holding in his left hand. "Red River Valley" didn't work at all, neither did

"The Battle Hymn of the Republic." But "Wild-wood Rose" seemed to do okay, so he softly sang:

> "Now listen you communists and niggers and
>   Jews,
> Tell all your buddies to spread the news."

Special Agent-in-Charge Alan Ward shifted un-easily behind the wheel of the Polara. He wasn't used to the heat, wasn't born to it like Anderson; he had even changed his white shirt at a gas sta-tion outside Winona, although the fresh one was soon as soaked as the first one. And this morning, while Anderson had stayed in the sack at the mo-tel in Batesville, the young agent had run three miles through the short-lived coolness of the July dawn. Anderson had shaken his head at the pant-ing, sweat-lathered man upon his return: that kind of radical physical activity was bound to eventually mess up a fellow's equilibrium, leaving him prey to all manners of nervous disorders. In Ander-son's experience there was but one justification to run anywhere—and that was to avoid incoming German shells. But young Ward, recently assigned to the Memphis field office after an extended convalescent leave for some reason, was a strange kid. He'd let slip something about his folks being strict Quakers.

> "Your day of judgment will soon be nigh,
> As the Lord in His Wisdom looks down from
>   on high."

Anderson, reverting to whistling as he mulled over the lyrics, peered out his side window again. Most of the tar-paper shanties were abandoned, with bluestem grass poking up through the cracks in the porch boards. Through the years, nearly all the white sharecroppers—like his own kin—had said to hell with futility and struck out for the cities, for lunch buckets and assembly lines and store-bought whiskey as smooth as a baby's ass. The few shanties that were still occupied belonged to the colored, who'd been liberated from slavery only to fall into another pit of servitude, the tenant-farming system.

Negroes, not colored anymore, he suddenly reminded himself, but it was hard to break old habits. And hell, what was a man if not a jumble of old habits, most of them bad?

Of course, young Ward wouldn't see it that way. He was straight out of Camelot boot camp—speaking those Bostonian *a*'s and saying "Cuber" instead of Cuba and all of that prissy folderol. Jesus, he even had that little flip of fair hair that kept falling down across his concerned brow, requiring him to decisively sweep it aside every couple of minutes or so. If he smiled at all it was to say: *I'm on to your antics, bub.*

All in all, precisely the wrong fellow to be headed into Mississippi with at the height of redneck summer. The Delta would eat him alive and spit out his college diploma.

"But ours is not to question why," Anderson muttered.

Ward asked, "What was that?"

"Nothing . . . just thinking."

"You finished going through that file yet?"

"Getting there, Boss."

Ward frowned, and Anderson looked outside again.

Nice woods now instead of just fields: pines,

sweet gums, fewer hickories than up north but still a couple scattered here and there. Out in the leaf-broken light he imagined that he could see a stocky kid with an octagonal-barreled .22 rifle, waiting breathlessly for a buck to pop up and flash his white rump patch as he hightailed it for fresh concealment.

Then Anderson's habitual smile faded.

If he peered deep enough into the shadows, he could conjure colder woods, snowy Belgian woods being crossed by a GI with strips of olive-drab blanket wrapped around his frozen boots. His lieutenant had once bragged to a visiting general that with an entire platoon of men like Pfc. Roop Anderson he could have kept the krauts from busting through the Ardennes in the first place. Bullshit, but he had learned what the federals had early in the Civil War: the average peckerwood was the most natural-born infantryman in the world. He could suffer both privation and awesome cruelty without ever losing his sunny disposition, a quality the Northerner usually mistook for insolence. But it wasn't. It was grit.

Yet, admittedly, his fellow Southerners could also dish out more cruelty than they'd ever been served.

Ward might not believe it, but Anderson had come home to the Hill country of Mississippi something of a rabble-rouser. It had not taken him and the other returned veterans long to figure out that in their absence, the local political machine had put a lock on the county—and damn near every job opportunity inside its borders.

When a former Marine complained about the situation and got beaten senseless with pickax handles for his trouble, Anderson got mad. He organ-

ized a pickax party of his own, and some of the
machine boys found themselves laid up for a while.
He then ran for sheriff and with the support of
the veterans won by two hundred votes, a comfortable margin in those times. He kept a clean
operation—at least by Mississippi standards. Two
terms and plenty of new enemies later, an agent
friend with the Memphis field office of the FBI
talked him into applying to the Bureau. Why not?
It amounted to tripling his paycheck.

That had been eleven years, four field offices,
several hundred thousand miles of travel, and a
busted marriage ago.

His watery gray eyes turned back to the lyrics:

> "Will His battle be lost by mixing the races?
> We want beautiful babies, not ones with brown
>   faces.
> Never, never, never, I say,
> For the Ku Klux Klan is here to stay."

He yawned, then said, "Well, I guess these Ku
Kluckers are better at lynchings than lyrics. Or
maybe you need somebody like Nat King Cole to
breathe some life into this tune. What do you
think?"

"Please just read the file, Mr. Anderson. I can
do without the cabaret." Using his left blinker like
a good boy should, Ward passed an overloaded
hay truck whose cargo filled the Dodge with a
miasma of sweet grasses. The smell lingered inside the car for some minutes.

Anderson hurriedly leafed through the rest of
the material. Nothing new or particularly interesting: the same old photographs of police German
shepherds treeing colored kids, of fire hoses bowl-

ing over protestors—the dirty linen of a South utterly mystified why the attention of the entire civilized world was suddenly focused on it. Dixie felt like the world was staring at it, and staring wasn't polite.

Anderson was smiling again as he riffled through the last of the stuff: the eight-by-ten photographs of the three missing volunteers of the Voter Education Project. But he wasn't thinking about the kids; he was considering his fledgling working relationship with the young man beside him.

Ward finally noticed the smile and asked, "Something tickling you, Mr. Anderson?"

"Sorta." He met Ward's eyes squarely. "You don't like me, do you, Boss?"

"I wouldn't say that."

"What would you say, then?"

Ward's look turned pensive. "I just don't share your sense of humor."

"Well, whatever kind you got, keep it. After enough years in this monkey suit, that's all you're left with." Anderson yawned again. Already the heat was slowing his metabolism, and here he was back in the state less than a day. Pretty soon he'd be moving as if the earth's gravity had doubled. Hell, maybe Mississippi had more gravity weighing on it than other states. Some states had damn near no gravity at all—like California. "How long you been with the Bureau, Boss?"

"Five years."

"Straight from college?"

"No, the Justice Department first."

"Oh, a Kennedy boy." Anderson chuckled, realizing that he was pushing Ward but also believing that now was the time to find out where things stood between them. With any luck Ward would back off, and Anderson would subtly take over the direction of the investigation—before the young agent got them both in muck over the tops of their waders. "Now I see," he said quietly, "now I see."

Ward kept his voice level, his gaze locked on the heat-shimmery highway. "Look, I don't know if you do see. But let's get this straight—"

"By all means, Boss."

"I haven't had pimples for years. I shave every morning. I even go to the can on my own. So you can quit sticking me with the 'boss' stuff, Anderson. They put me in charge of this one because I've been through this same gig before."

"Birmingham, then? Or Montgomery?"

"Oxford. I was with Meredith when he enrolled at Old Miss."

Closing his eyes, Anderson rested his head on the back of the seat. "This won't be any college-town social. Not down here in Delta country."

"Oxford was a social?"

"Well, so you got roughed by some good old boys who usually save that stuff for the gridiron or Halloween—"

"No, I got shot in the shoulder."

Anderson bit his lip, then opened his eyes on a crossroads store. It could have been plunked down into any Mississippi county and assumed to have always been there—a grimy front window through which a slab of salted pork was dimly visible, a R.C. Cola ice chest on the sagging wooden porch, and beside it an aged idler in a wicker-bottom chair tilted back against the paintless clapboards.

"Well," he said after a long silence between them, "at least you lived through Oxford, Mr. Ward. That's the important thing."

"No, James Meredith lived—that's the important thing."

Anderson wanted to roll his eyes. A guy who talked like this would have lasted all of a day on the front line. But something had indeed been settled. Ward was not about to release his purchase on the reins. Not yet. So Anderson grinned, scratched his belly, and asked, "Know what has four eyes and can't see worth a shit?"

"What?"

"Mississippi."

Ward laughed a little.

Main Street, also the state highway, emptied into a square with a heat-bald lawn and a flowering magnolia in each corner. At one in the afternoon the benches were empty, but a dog that might have been part beagle was sleeping on the shaded floor of the gazebo.

Alan Ward parked on the north side of the quad, in front of the courthouse. It looked like it had been built for a town ten times the size of this one: three stories of brick with forty-foot Ionic columns in front which suggested that Greek Revival had been the architect's stylistic intention. Yet the white paint of the cupola was chipping, and its copperclad roof had turned as green as moss.

Two crows or ravens—Ward had no idea which—were perched on the weathervane, seemingly hunkered down in their shiny black feathers against the heat.

"Lock your door," Anderson said as they were getting out.

"I know. I've been here before."

"Easy there, Boss." Anderson gave that disingenuous Southern grin of his and slipped into his wrinkled jacket.

Ward had not wanted the fifty-year-old special agent on this assignment with him. Anderson had a well-deserved reputation as a kiss-off, a sleep-walker, even a shirker—unless something in the mechanics or the ambience of the case happened to strike his unfathomable fancy and energize him until his more natural sloth had its way again. Also, Ward had not cared for Anderson's insinuation that he required an Indian guide for this neck of the woods. He had fought over his turf, lain bleeding on it, so he didn't need some wisecracking peckerwood to tell him what drums beating in the hot stillness of the night meant.

"Care to pay your respects?" Anderson asked. Smiling as usual, he was pointing at the bronze statue of a Confederate soldier guarding the front of courthouse. The big guano-splattered hands were clasping the muzzle of the musket, and the pitted eyes had such a distant cast to them they seemed focused on the Gulf of Mexico, a hundred miles to the south.

" 'Course," Anderson went on, "Johnny never dressed that good. He woulda thought he'd died and gone to heaven if he'd had a greatcoat that fine. But don't tell the Daughters of the Confederacy that."

"I doubt I could tell them anything."

Anderson chuckled, and Ward scanned the placard: the usual florid crap about Asleep in Eternal Honor for Their Glorious Sacrifice in the Struggle for Southern Independence. Naturally, not a hint of apology for maintaining that "peculiar institution," as slavery had been called in polite company, or for forcing the bloodiest war in American history. It irked him more than anything else about them: how unrepentant they were. If he had his way, to every one of these Rebel memorials a placard would be attached, honoring the 38,000 Negro soldiers who'd died in Union service. "Your people fight in that?" he asked.

Anderson just nodded, but for once he wasn't smiling.

The courthouse front doors must have been eight feet tall, half tiger-stripe oak and half glass that had ripples of faint iridescence in it. The brass-plated latch Anderson grasped had been worn down to the underlying iron.

"After you, Boss."

Ward glared at him as he passed into the relative coolness of a long marble corridor. Midway down it, a Negro janitor with a wizened face was mopping the floor. He looked like he wanted to tell them to mind where they stepped, but was afraid to.

"Is it okay to walk through?" Ward asked, his voice echoing.

"Yes, suh," he answered without much conviction.

"What you saying there?" Anderson asked jovially, ambling past with his hands in his pockets.

"Fine, suh . . . just fine."

Ward suspected that had he not been along Anderson would have called the old man "boy."

They halted in front of a door with SHERIFF'S OFFICE painted in black and gold letters on the pebbled glass. Behind the rough, transparent surface he could discern no movement.

Again Anderson made a to-do of opening the door for him. "Boss?"

"I'm also tall enough to reach door handles, Mr. Anderson."

The older agent nodded as if he were making a mental note of the fact.

Inside, a deputy in his late thirties was manning the front desk. He had pulled out the typewriter board and rested his badly scuffed Acme boots on it. Scowling, he was reading a copy of the *Delta Democrat-Times,* the most liberal paper in the state—which may have accounted for the scowl.

"Good afternoon, my name is Alan Ward. FBI."

The deputy lowered the newspaper to have a look at the two men, but said nothing. A coil of his oily hair hung down almost between his disinterested eyes; his sunken cheeks had been cratered by acne.

Ward produced his ID. "I said, Deputy Alan Ward—FBI."

"That Federal Bureau of Integration?" Smirking at his own joke, the deputy took a pack of Pall Malls from his bulging uniform shirt pocket and lit up. Ward had been around enough local cops to realize that most, in the interests of looking professional, tucked their smokes in their socks. The deputy's indolent eyes made a slow pass over the nearly identical business suits of the agents. "In them getups, you fellas ain't exactly under cover, are you, now?"

"We're here to see Sheriff Stuckey," Ward said.

"Bad time to catch him. He's busy."

"We'll wait."

"Might want to come back another time."

"Like when?"

"Can't say. He's been real busy."

"We'll wait."

"Suit yourself."

If only to calm down, Ward began strolling around the reception area of the office. The ceiling fan was warbling like it needed oil. He could feel the deputy's gaze on him and tried to ignore it. In a fly-specked glass case were hundreds of law-enforcement shoulder patches from all over the country. He was surprised to find one from his hometown PD in New Hampshire.

Whispering brought his attention back to the front desk. Anderson's face was inches from the deputy's, his knuckles resting on the desk blotter as he leaned toward the man. Ward couldn't catch all of what the agent was telling the man, but he did hear: ". . . Listen, you illiterate fuck, you tote your ass—and the remaining ten percent of you—insides there and get Stuckey. If that play don't meet with your approval, I'd like very much to open the sheriff's door with your head."

Ward wasn't sure if the deputy's shocked expression came more from Anderson's threat or from hearing an unexpected Mississippi accent.

Nevertheless, the young agent said severely, "Mr. Anderson."

Again that infuriating grin: "Yes, Mr. Ward?"

At that instant the door marked SHERIFFF RAYMOND STUCKEY glided open, and a huge man sauntered out holding an empty coffee mug at his side. Although in rumpled civilian dress, he wore a pearl-handled automatic in a cross-draw holster on his belt.

"Oh," he said as if pleasantly surprised, "I see we got company, Clinton."

"Yes, sir."

"Looks like a couple Hoover boys come a-calling, what now? Well, we been expecting you gentlemen. I'm Ray Stuckey and I assume you met my deputy, Mr. Pell."

Anderson was standing closer to the sheriff, so he shook hands first. "Rupert Anderson."

Stuckey seemed as taken aback by the accent—or lack of one to him—as Pell had been, but then his eyes seemed to narrow in recollection. "*Roop* Anderson?"

"Heard of me?"

"This and that through the years."

Ward had to introduce himself.

"Pleasure," Stuckey said reflexively, then added, "So you boys are down here to help us with our nigra problems, hah?"

Ward was eager to hit that one head-on, but before he could answer Anderson said—far too agreeably to suit the young agent—"No, Sheriff, we're just working a plainy old missing-persons case."

Stuckey hung his mug on a wall rack, then started back for his office. "Well, in that case, let's talk, Anderson." He hooked his thumb at Ward. "You want your boy in on this?"

Anderson was trying not to smile.

Ward took a deep breath. "I'm in charge of this investigation, Sheriff. And it might be a bit more serious than a 'plainy old missing persons.' "

"Might or is?" Stuckey asked, shutting the door behind them.

"I guess we'll find out."

While Ward sank into one side of a worn leather sofa, Anderson examined the framed photographs on the wall. Among those of Stuckey embracing various state officials and George Wallace from neighboring Alabama was one of the sheriff in a straw panama, holding up a large sunfish.

"Y'all got some dandy bream down this way, don't you, now?" Anderson asked.

A little pride seeped out of the sheriff's eyes. "We got us a few."

"I prefer them to cats."

"Me too. No muddy taste like we got in most our catfish."

"What about your—?"

"Sheriff," Ward interrupted, "what can you tell us about your investigation into the disappearance of these three subjects?"

Stuckey looked offended by the Magnolia State amenities being cut short, but Ward didn't give a damn. He wasn't here to win friends.

"I got nothing to add to what I told both your Memphis and New Orleans offices, Mr. Ward."

"You mean that in all the days since then you've obtained no further information?"

"That's about the size of it," Stuckey said.

"But interviews were attempted, certainly."

"Most certainly."

"May I see copies of the reports indicating the dates and times of those attempts?"

"Why? I just said we got nothing out of them, Mr. Ward.'"

"Still, I'd like to see them."

Stuckey chortled under his breath. His eyes flickered toward Anderson for support before he turned back to Ward. "I woulda thought your partner acquainted you with how things are run down here."

"Meaning, Sheriff?" Ward asked.

"Well, we don't see how much paper we can cram in the file cabinets."

"Are you telling me there's no record of these attempted interviews?"

"I'm telling you we pursued all leads as we saw fit—and didn't come up with a goddamn thing, son." For the first time there was anger in Stuckey's broad face. "If you ask me, it's all a mess of publicity crap dreamed up by that Martin Luther Coon over in Atlanta! *That*," he shouted, slapping his desktop for even more emphasis, "is where your investigation oughta be headed, not on some teenage vagrants who're most likely safe and sound somewheres up north at this very minute!"

"Sheriff, if I might ask—"

"Now, son, you tell me something. Is the Federal Bureau of Investigation charged with looking into communist agitation?"

"Agitation is a rather loose definition for legal purposes."

The veins in Stuckey's neck started standing out, and Anderson looked out the window. "Don't you go splitting hairs with me, mister! I know damn well what Hoover should and shouldn't be doing! Get him away from Washington, and he'd admit it, too! Now, you trace this disappearance hoopla back to its source, I guarantee you're gonna find communist seed money! You can tell old J. Edgar for Raymond Lamont Stuckey to take the blinders off and start hunting for communist money! You hear me?"

2

As soon as Ward and he reached the bottom of the courthouse steps, Rupert Anderson looked about for thunderheads. And sure enough, big ones were building in the north over the Hill country, although they were too distant to promise any relief here.

Ward began fishing in his trouser pocket for his keys at least twenty steps away from the Dodge.

He hadn't said a word since leaving Sheriff Stuckey's office, but Anderson was willing to bet that the young agent would get on a self-righteous roll as soon as they got inside the privacy of the car. So he decided to beat him to the punch: "You did a dandy job in there, Boss."

Ward paused, holding his door half open. He recoiled as the hot air trapped inside the sedan flowed up around his face like flames. "What're you saying?"

Anderson hiked his shoulders.

Ward waited another moment for an answer, then angrily got in behind the wheel, which he found too sunbaked to grasp right away.

Anderson gently knocked on the window of his yet locked door.

Ward reached over and snapped up the button. "I asked you a question, Mr. Anderson."

"And what was that, Boss?" he asked blandly, getting in.

"Cut the crap!" Ward barked, his little forelock falling across his eyes, requiring the Kennedyesque swipe of his right hand to put it back in place. "Whichever way you look at it, Stuckey's going to obstruct our efforts." He fired the engine and backed out of the parking space much too fast.

"That's true."

Ward shot a sideward glance at him, but then seemed to settle down some. He drove around the square, the government Dodge drawing glowers from the townies braving the heat, and then rejoined the highway to head south out of town. When he finally spoke again, it was with the cool, self-controlled voice of a supervisor who prides himself on never losing his temper. "What's your beef, Mr. Anderson? I'd really like to know. Please explain yourself."

"Well, Raymond Lamont Stuckey had two ways to mess with us. The first was from the sidelines—"

"Enough of the football analogies."

"I like football," Anderson said.

"So do I, but just get to the point."

"Point is, from the sidelines old Stuckey woulda been content to hoot and holler at us. Chickenshit bickering that won't amount to nothing in the course of the game."

Ward said in his gravest voice: "This isn't a game, Mr. Anderson."

"The devil it isn't. Follow the rules or lose yardage. And you just broke the first rule: thou shall not patronize the folks in power down here. Now

Stuckey's taking it damn personal when there's no need for him to—"

"So at this point he's going to trot out onto the playing field and mix it up with us?"

"You got it, Boss. But watch the football analogies."

Ward ignored the gibe. "Just let Stuckey try."

Anderson looked at the young agent disbelievingly. "Oh, he will—trust me. Ray Stuckey sure as shit will. And he's got more boys on his team than we do."

"What, one deputy?"

"No, every white male in this county. Oh, Ray Stuckey was a dandy fella to piss off royal."

Suddenly Ward laughed. "And what about your cordial exchange with Deputy Pell?"

"What?" Anderson asked, genuinely mystified. "I wasn't patronizing Pell."

"Maybe not, but threatening to ram his noggin through Stuckey's door doesn't exactly strike me as getting along with the natives."

"That was just joshing."

"Joshing?"

"You bet—posturing, clearing the bad air between us. He knew that. The thing is, I wasn't putting myself above him. Stuckey neither."

"Oh," Ward said derisively, "I'll go along with that."

Anderson lowered his voice: "There's a point here, Ward. One that will help you get the job done. And that's the only reason we're down here—to get a particular job done." Then he took a pack of spearmint gum out of his inner jacket pocket, wishing that it were chewing tobacco, which he'd sworn off the day he joined the Bureau because field offices didn't come equipped with spittoons, and popped a stick of gum into his dry mouth. He was finished talking for a while.

So was Ward.

The modest houses on the outskirts gave way to fields with an occasional cabin at the end of an unpaved drive. The cotton was about a foot high, ready for its last hoeing before picking time in late August. Bad feelings with a partner didn't rest easy with Anderson, and he was thinking of talking a little cotton with Ward, but one glance at the young man's lock-jawed expression decided him against it.

About a mile from town Ward turned off the highway, once again using his signal although there wasn't another car in sight, and started up a red dirt road. The Dodge tossed up a rooster tail of dust that, when Anderson looked back, was sifting through the sun-scorched Indian grass like smoke.

"Mount Zion First Baptist," Ward explained when they had reached the crown of the hill.

"Glory," Anderson said, climbing out. He stretched a kink out of the small of his back.

In the distance, one of the windows of the courthouse cupola was glinting like a mirror. A stench of charcoal hung in the air, not a good charcoal smell like that of a barbecue but a biting stink that spoke of destruction.

He followed Ward toward a pile of gray and white ashes from which charred beams jutted like ribs. The blackened wood had a texture like alligator skin—some hot fire.

"The three civil-rights kids," Ward said quietly, as if it were still a church, "came here hoping to set up a voter-registration clinic. The congregation didn't even get a chance to say yes or no or even maybe before the Klan burned them down."

Anderson held his tongue about this.

"The morning after, the three kids came back to apologize to the preacher and his wife."

"How do you know this?"

"Transcript of Memphis's original telephone conversation with Stuckey. Wasn't it in the file I gave you?"

"Nope," Anderson said.

"Well, maybe it's in my personal materials."

"Personal materials?"

"Just some things I was going through last night at the motel," Ward said irritably. "You'll see them."

Anderson exhaled—he had lived with it countless times before: the boss withholding this or that just so he could have a little something in reserve to bolster the pretense that he was, after all, the goddamned boss. "What else did Stuckey have to say?"

"Not much, believe me. From here, the kids went down the road"—Ward pointed south, where the highway vanished into the wavering of an asphalt mirage—"dropping by at the houses of people in the congregation. I guess that's where we roll up our sleeves and start."

"Start?" Anderson was grinning again.

"Yes, that's where we kick off our investigation. I presume you've done one before?"

"Enough of them to know these folks won't say squat to a couple of outsiders wearing monkey suits and arriving in a brand-new Dodge Polara. They'd bite off their tongues and swallow them first."

"That remains to be seen." Ward had already started back for the car.

Anderson lingered a moment, studying the ruin, but mostly thinking that he should have transferred back to the St. Louis office last winter when he'd had the chance. Then he turned for the car, whose engine Ward had already started.

"What was on your mind back there?" Ward asked a minute later as he turned onto the highway.

"How's that?" Anderson said, although he knew full well what the young agent wanted to hear— some reassuring liberal sorghum about what an awful shame the burning had been. Burning was his favorite theme; he had even code-named the file for this investigation "Mississippi Burning."

"What were you thinking when you were looking over what's left of Mount Zion Baptist?"

"Just that some kids came along promising them the means to vote, and when the kids were gone these folks still had no vote, plus no place to go on Sunday. That's progress, I suppose, now. Wouldn't you say?"

"You might want to go up this drive fast, Boss. Bail out fast too. I should probably go around back to cut off any skedaddlers."

"Why? These people have nothing to hide."

"Fine," Anderson snapped, sitting back to enjoy the sharp rocking of the Polara over the rutted driveway. It cut through a thicket of wild holly, the tender spring leaves now withered, and finally opened onto a loop on whose far curve a pig farm stood.

A Negro man could be seen standing out in the maze of pigsties, sprinkling feed to a dozen or so skinny chickens, his lips moving like he was singing to himself.

Ward got out and smoothed down his tie before walking toward the pens.

Grunting, Anderson left the car a moment later,

but then leaned against the fender as the young
agent bounded over the first jerry-built fence with
Hyannisport vigor and called out, "Excuse me!
Excuse me, sir!"

Anderson chuckled as the man dropped his burlap feed sack and began striding away from the
agent and into the swiftly closing Mississippi sun-
set. It might well be dark before Ward could make
his way back.

"May I talk to you a minute, sir?" Ward was
now trotting through the mud after him, vaulting
over the fences with admirable ease. Unfortunately,
there were no pigs to impede him. Maybe the
Negro had proved no good at raising them. There
was a lot more to it than just slopping the lazy
brutes. Or maybe he'd been too good at raising
pigs—and then given the word that it was best for
his health if he stopped showing up his white
neighbors. Anderson had seen it before; most colored would work like demons if it was on their
own land. Whatever had happened here, it had
been recent: the pens were still muddy and the
corncrib looked in pretty good repair.

He thought of taking over feeding the chickens
for the man if only because they were making a
mess of the split bag. But he looked at the mud
and then at his polished oxfords and decided no.

"Sir!" Ward's voice came from the dim sweet-
gum woods on the far side of the farm.

"Just stop sometimes before you reach the Big
Muddy, Boss. That old boy's gonna dance across
the river like a water skipper and you'll sink like a
stone," Anderson said, taking off his jacket to use
as a pillow. Then he climbed up, using the bumper,
and sprawled across the warm hood of the Dodge.

The stars and the crickets came out about the same time.

Ward returned twenty minutes or so later with black gumbo caked all over his shoes.

"How'd the interview go, Boss?"

Without a word Ward jumped inside the Dodge and slammed shut his door.

Anderson slid down off the hood and entered by his door. "You about ready to find a motel?"

"Hell no, night's young."

"Just what I was thinking," Anderson said, grinning despite his exasperation with a man who didn't know when to call it a day.

It was hard to believe that people still lived this way.

No electricity. The only illumination in the single-room cabin came from a hurricane lamp on the table, and the yellowish glow was drawing in every night insect between the Mississippi and the Yazoo. Among them flitted a disturbing number of mosquitoes, which was understandable when Alan Ward recalled from Anderson's and his arrival how the cabin was situated on the bank of a weedy slough. So far he had sustained five or six bites, but Anderson sat across the table from him apparently unmolested, his smiling face waxy-looking in the lamplight.

The old Negro woman with the shrunken torso and bandy legs had risen some minutes ago to make them coffee. But after rattling around her graniteware atop the wood cookstove and rummaging through the wall-mounted apple crate that served as her pantry, she confessed that she really had no coffee.

"That's all right, Hattie," Ward said, urging her to sit again.

Her husband lay silent on a surplus army cot in the corner farthest from the light. She had introduced the agents to him by passing the lamp over his face. It was horribly bruised and swollen, the deep purple of eggplant, and his eyes had lit but briefly on the strange white faces before growing bleary again.

"Do you understand why we're here, Hattie?" Ward asked as soon as she was seated again.

"Why you here?" She looked puzzled, perhaps thinking that knowing the reason would be taken as prying. "No, suh."

"Special Agent Anderson and I are here to help you and Mose. To make sure that what happened won't happen again. Do you understand now, Hattie?"

She didn't respond. Her eyes had gone still in her wrinkled face.

Ward wanted to explain so much more, to win her trust, but then he caught the contemptuous expression on Anderson's paraffin like face. "Hattie, were you in the church when it was set afire?"

She hesitated. "Yes, suh."

"Was Mose there, too?"

She nodded, then turned as her husband began softly moaning. "Don't you worry none, Mose. You want a sup of water?" He gave no answer, but she rose anyway and got him a drink.

"And you two started for home? Is that right?"

"Yes, suh," she said from beside the cot.

"And you were stopped by two white men?"

Mose murmured something to her, and she whispered something back.

"I asked you, Hattie," Ward went on, "if you were stopped by two white men."

"Yes, suh."

"And these two white men attacked your husband?"

"They cussed Mose bad."

"All right, but did they beat him as well?"

Another troubled pause. "Yes, suh."

"Can you identify these men?"

"No, suh."

Anderson was tinkering with the lamp flame as if oblivious to the interview.

"Were these men wearing hoods or masks of any sort, Hattie?"

"No, suh."

"And you still can't identify them?"

"No, suh."

"Can we assume then they weren't from these parts?"

"Don't know, sir."

Ward slowly let out a breath. "Did you report this incident to the sheriff?"

"Sheriff Stuckey, suh?"

"Yes."

She had returned the ladle to the water bucket and was now fiddling with a string of cheap red beads dangling off a square nail. Beside it hung a black hat with a lace veil. These were the finishing touches to her church wear, Ward supposed, waiting for her answer. "Did you tell Sheriff Stuckey or any of his men, Hattie?"

"No, suh."

"Why not?"

Anderson gave him a hard look, and Ward changed his question: "But you told all this to the three civil-rights boys when they came around to apologize, didn't you?"

"Yes, suh."

"They must have been pretty discouraged, what?"

"Yes, suh."

"Did they say where they were going next?"

"No, suh."

Ward came to his feet. Through the screenless window he could make out the stagnant waters of the slough, silvery in the faint starlight. Frogs were beginning to grumble. "Well, thank you, Hattie." He swatted a mosquito that was whining near his ear. "Thank you very much."

Rising, Anderson complimented her church hat, and for the first time the old woman smiled.

3

"Great day in the morning," Rupert Anderson yawned. Before the windshield lay the town square with the gazebo and the magnolias throwing long shadows across the grass. Ward had his notes propped up against the horn bar of the steering wheel and was going through a kind of briefing for the upcoming day.

Anderson was dying for a cup of coffee.

"Around fifteen hundred hours that afternoon," Ward said, "Deputy Pell claims he arrested the three boys for speeding." He glanced up from his papers, his brow furrowed. "All three of them for speeding? Not just the driver?"

Anderson chuckled knowingly. "Hell, the three of them was doing the same exact speed, hah?"

Ward shook his head. "Pell held them in jail until twenty-two hundred hours that night, then released them. They drove off. He says he followed them as far as the county line and never saw them again."

Anderson's drowsy attention was drawn to the front doors of the courthouse, through which Sheriff Stuckey and Deputy Pell had just ambled, damn near arm in arm. They started down the steps, but stopped every three or so to give full sway to their animated conversation. "Just look at that sad-sack peckerwood," Anderson mumbled.

"Who?" Ward asked, clearly not appreciating the break in his train of thought.

"Old Clinton Pell there." The deputy wore his black basket-weave gunbelt askew so that his holster sagged halfway down his thigh. "Guess these boys never heard of keepers."

"What're keepers?"

"Little leather straps that help keep your Sam Browne belt from wearing like a goddamn Hula Hoop."

"Why didn't they make a phone call?"

"Who?"

"Who else? The three civil-rights kids."

"Oh," Anderson said, still tracking the slow progress of the sheriff and the deputy down the steps and across the square. "Why should they?"

"These kids were trained activists. They're taught to check in periodically. And if arrested, they're supposed to call the minute they're released from custody. Their hotel—Negro clientele—is five, maybe six minutes south of town. They should've phoned from there. It doesn't make sense that they didn't."

"Who can say what a kid's gonna do?"

Stuckey parted company with Pell on the sidewalk across the street from the southern edge of the square. The sheriff doffed his panama in greeting at the door to the barbershop, then stepped inside, vanishing into the cool-looking shadows of the place. A couple of doors down the street, Pell was talking to a woman—arguing was more like it.

Anderson found himself watching her more than him. She had long white arms and one of those lustrous complexions that comes from a lifetime of avoiding the sun. Even at this distance he could tell that she had a face that could still turn heads, although he also sensed that in the past year or so, she'd had come into her first fading. There was something sweetly plaintive, haunting even, about those first laugh lines showing up in a woman's beauty.

Pell suddenly grabbed her forearm, not terribly roughly but hard enough to make her shake free and walk quickly away. She was wearing a pink uniform, which made sense when she disappeared into the beauty salon at the corner.

Pell, looking around to assess how much his dignity had suffered, then laughed it all off and joined his boss in the barbershop.

"The civil-rights office in Yazoo," Ward droned on in that ain't-this-fishy tone of voice of his, "started calling the moment they didn't check in as scheduled. The sheriff told them he had no idea where the three young men were. And there is the first lie."

"Where? From the sheriff or the civil-rights office?"

Ward eyed him. "Who would you believe, Mr. Anderson?"

"I'd just go easy about calling a Mississippi sheriff a liar, Mr. Ward."

"Is that because you were one?"

Anderson wanted to slap the smirk off Ward's face. Instead he focused on the small Stars and Bars hanging in the barbershop window. "Let me give you the big picture, Boss—"

"Please do."

"I know you don't think much of these cracker lawmen down here. Think they're ignorant bigots with one hand around a mint julep and another around a bullwhip to keep the darkies in line. But when Kennedy wanted to take the West Virginia primary, who did he turn to, Mr. Ward? The clergy? The college deans? Not on your life. He turned to the high sheriffs with his fucking hat in his hand. And there ain't but a handful of these old boys Lyndon Baines don't know on a first-name basis. Hell, he even knows the names of their favorite hunting dogs. See now, he *has* to tread lightly around them, what if he expects to live in the same house come four years. So I ask you, Mr. Ward, what does the president of these United States know that you don't?"

Ward stared back at him for a long moment, then said, "Let's get something to eat."

What Anderson had said about the power of Southern sheriffs was disturbingly true, Ward admitted to himself as he stood with the middle-aged agent, waiting to be seated in the small, crowded diner. But he was not about to be intimidated by one, and so far the Bureau had done a good job of thwarting any "end runs" these officials had sent through Congress and the Justice Department to hobble Special Agent Ward's mischief making in their completely law-abiding jurisdictions. Still, it was a real fear that awoke him some nights: that these forays into the medieval South for the sake of justice would be brought to a crashing halt by political pressure.

"We're full right up, honey," the waitress said to Anderson, who'd been stealing glances at her decent enough legs during her last few trips up and down the aisle. "You all wanna wait an itty bit?"

"Is the wait worth it?"

"We ain't full for nothing, honey. Want a menu while you're waiting?"

Ward realized that most of the men in the place were staring at Anderson and him. One by one, he glared back at them, almost enjoying their sudden discomfort.

The waitress must have noticed this exchange, for she said sotto voce, "Don't take no offense, son. Mean and ignorant, every last one of them. Especially when they're eating. Something about eating brings out the meanness in some men. So what you all going to do? Wait or leave?"

"Wait," Anderson said in so sugary a voice Ward had to turn away: Mississippi-style flirtation was a bit too cloying for his taste. "Just to be near you."

But she ate it up and laughed merrily as she rushed to take the coffeepot around.

Ward noticed two empty swivel seats at the far end of the narrow room. "What about down there?"

Anderson smiled uneasily, then said under his breath, "Colored."

"So?"

"Don't even think about it, Mr. Ward." Anderson gestured at a nearby booth. "Look, these folks are almost done. They're waiting on their check—"

But Ward had already started down the aisle, feeling the curious stares on his back as if they were hot pokers. Forcing himself to smile, he took the seat beside a young negro in denim workclothes. "Good morning. I'm Alan Ward." He offered his hand.

The Negro declined to shake it, but did mumble, "Hollis Johnson, suh."

Ward slipped the menu from its clip on the back of the chrome napkin holder and examined it, even though the words and numbers were only blur. He fully realized that the place had gone silent. Anderson was still waiting beside the cash register, his face crimson.

"Things sure have been crazy around here, what, Hollis?"

The man was staring down into his coffee cup as if waiting for some answer to this unexpected predicament to bubble to the surface. "I got nothing to say, suh."

"There's nothing to be afraid of."

Then Hollis Johnson looked at him with what seemed like hatred, as if the fear had filled him with hate. "I said I got nothing to say, suh." With that, he took a dollar out of the front pocket of his faded jeans, tucked it under the edge of his plate, and left.

Ward saw that the Negro had only started his breakfast.

Fennis Johnson was resting on the splintery porch steps with his elbows propped on the highest step, his buttocks on the middle one, and his small, leathery heels on the lowest. He was waiting for a moon in a desultory kind of way, although he had no certainty one would swell out of Alabama tonight. There weren't so many stars like some nights, but he could see enough of them to put the idea of trying to count them out of his head. Counting stars was useless business, his brother Hollis said.

Some nights like this, warm and still, he liked to borrow Hollis's flashlight and gallivant down among the reeds, hunting for frogs and mud puppies and whatever else slithered along. But tonight he was content to sit.

Then a bright flickering down along the slough caught his eye.

Headlamps.

A faint road ran on either side of the snaking marsh. On the far bank, it was no matter if a car came or went: any crossing was a long ways off. And most the time it was white boys hunting for frogs to gig.

But this car—a GMC pickup truck—was traveling on the near side of the slough, going faster than what somebody would go who was listening for big frogs.

Fennis sat straight, wondering what to do.

Hollis, tired from his day's work down at the sawmill, had told him over supper not to bother him on any account.

Holding his breath, Fennis waited to see what the driver of the pickup would do at the junction with what everybody around here called Johnson Road. "Dang." He had turned up it, his two round headlamps sweeping over the tops of the horse-sugar bushes and before fixing on the shack.

Fennis had to squinch against the bright light.

The driver parked a ways down the slope: Fennis heard the ratchety sound when he set the parking brake. Two men got out of the GMC and started walking up.

"Fennis," one of them called out like he was mad or disgusted, "Hollis here?"

"Yes, suh, but he sleeping."

"Wake him up. Tell him we want to see him."

Fennis was afraid to ask, but also sensed that it was the thing to do: "Why?"

"Never mind, now. Just wake him up."

"Yes, suh." Fennis turned to fetch Hollis, but he already stood in the yawning front door, tucking his shirttail into his pants. He was blinking against the headlamps, probably trying to figure out who the two ofays were and why they'd come.

But then something frightful must have come into Hollis's mind, for he spun around and ran through the shack toward the back, spilling over something that broke with a crash in the little kitchen.

The two white men split up, each going around a side of the shack, and Fennis soon heard one of them holler that the nigger was doubling back toward the slough. This shout was no sooner echoing in the woods than Hollis came into sight, breathing hard like he'd been running all night, and jumped into the sty on his way down the slope, maybe figuring that the ofays wouldn't chase him through the gumbo and the squealing pigs.

But one of the white men, the biggest one, was waiting for Hollis on the down side of the pen and hugged him around the middle like in football. Hollis and he tumbled onto the grass, and from then on Fennis could see a fist working like it had a hammer in it, rising and falling against the shine of the headlamps.

"You got him?" the other ofay cried, coming at a lope.

"Hah! I got him!"

"Hold him!"

"I got him good!"

Then Hollis sprang up—he was strong, Hollis—and looked like he might get away. Somebody was screaming for him to do it, and after a few seconds Fennis realized that he himself was the one screaming. He was crying too, because he could feel the tears on his face, tickling his upper lip.

Yet as Hollis was scrambling up the slope on all fours, the second ofay kicked him in the face.

He went down again and didn't make a sound.

For a while the ofays stood over him, hands on their hips, spitting and panting like they were half sick from all the work Hollis had given them. But then each of them took one of Hollis's floppy legs and dragged him over to the pickup.

Over the years, "home" had been reduced to a water glass wrapped in a paper, a small ice bucket, and a pint of Jim Beam. Not that Roop Anderson had become a drunk. Mr. Hoover no more tolerated drunkenness than he did anything but snow-white shirts. But these articles had become the things Anderson looked forward to as the day wound down, just as another man might look forward to his wife, pipe, and newspaper. Anderson no longer had a wife; she'd gone her own way two years after he joined the Bureau. As far as a pipe, his appetite for tobacco had proved so compelling he'd quit every form of it when he finally found the strength to put down cigarettes. And newspapers tended to infuriate him, particularly after reading the accounts of incidents he'd been a party to—and couldn't recognize in the writing a kernel of the truth he'd seen with his own eyes.

With eyes closed, he savored another sip of bourbon.

Special Agent-in-Charge Ward could be heard on the floor, drinking a sodie through a straw, rustling through files even though it was a quarter to eleven and Anderson had twice suggested that they turn in.

A momentary silence made Anderson glance at Ward. He was studying the mugshot of one of the missing kids. The Jewish one from New Jersey, who wore a beatnik-looking goatee.

"You admire those people, don't you?"

"Don't you?" Ward said without looking up.

"I think they're being used."

The young agent frowned. "How's that?"

"Well, they're being fired up and sent down here in their sneakers just to get their heads cracked open."

"Maybe they believe in what they're doing."

"Do they believe they might wind up dead?" Anderson asked, realizing for the first time that, deep down, this is what he believed had happened to the three kids. But he didn't want to suggest anything of the sort to Ward.

"Perhaps they knew. Some things are worth dying for."

Anderson chuckled. "Down here they see it different." He pointed at Ward's soda bottle. "Let me spice that up for you, Boss. You'll go toothless drinking that sweet piss."

Ward looked like he was going to balk, but then handed it over. "How's it different, then?"

"For these people, some things are worth killing for." Anderson circled his fist around the lip of the Coke bottle, forming a funnel, and poured a healthy dose of Jim Beam into it. "Here, this'll put it all in perspective for you."

"Thanks," Ward said. "And that's what I'm trying to do, you know."

"Hah?"

"Understand it. Understand where all this blind hatred comes from."

Anderson licked the bourbon off his hand, thinking. "When I was a kid, there was a"—he paused, suddenly remembering not to say 'colored'—"a

Negro farmer down the road from us. Name of Monroe. His family was just casuals—"

"What's that?" Ward didn't wince when he took a slug of the spiked Coca-Cola; Anderson was somewhat disappointed.

"Casuals is the lowest kind of farm laborer. They don't even get paid in money. Just something called 'hand's share'—enough corn or peanuts or potatoes to keep them going. Well, Monroe was no lazy man. No sir. He worked his way up to a bona fide farm laborer, which meant maybe sixty cents a day. From there he became subtenant to a sharecropper, working the poorest acres of land this white fella had to rent to him. And finally Monroe became a full tenant, just like my daddy." Anderson took a mouthful of Jim Beam and smiled as he held it in his cheeks before swallowing. "Maybe Monroe was just luckier than my daddy. But it's hard to figure it that way—colored farmer could never get the same price for his bales as us. Anyways, he musta had a couple good years. He bought himself a mule." When Anderson saw that the significance of this was lost on Ward, he added, "Which was one helluva a big deal around town, because some of the white croppers didn't have one. My daddy among them."

"How'd your father feel about that?"

"He hated that goddamn mule. All his friends joshed him about it. Told him how they'd seen old Monroe and his mule out plowing, looking proud as cavalry. How Monroe was renting another quarter section on account of how well that mule was working out for him." Anderson stared off through the dingy wallpaper, then shook off the reverie that had taken hold of him, and had an another drink. "Then one morning that mule was dead.

Someone had poisoned its water trough. And after that, nobody mentioned that mule around my daddy. It just never came up again. Except once, a couple months later. He and I were walking down the road. A nice spring morning. We passed Monroe's place, and it was empty. Monroe had moved out. Gone North or something. Well, I looked up and caught my daddy smiling at those unplowed fields already going to weeds—and I knew that he'd done it. And he saw that I knew. He was ashamed." Anderson smiled again, but sadly now. "At least I believed he was ashamed. And he turned to me and said, 'If you're not better than a nigger, who the devil are you better'n?'"

"You think that's an excuse?" Ward asked after a few seconds.

"No, not an excuse. It's just a story."

"Every story's supposed to have a moral."

"You think so?"

"Yes, I do."

"Then you just haven't lived enough stories."

Ward shrugged. "Might be, but where does this story leave you?"

"With an old man so eaten up with hate he didn't even know it was poverty that was killing him." Yawning, Anderson swung his legs over the side of his bed and began rolling down his black socks. He realized that Ward was staring at the scars, the missing little toe on his right foot.

"What happened?—if I might ask."

"Another story without a moral. Feet froze pretty bad. The Ardennes." Anderson thought to wash his socks before calling it a day, but then said to hell with one more minor chore and stuffed them inside his shoes. He was going to ask Ward if it would be all right if he turned off the lights anytime soon—when the windows exploded and shards of glass skipped all around the room.

"Christ!" Ward cried, rolling against his bed and reaching under the pillow for his revolver.

Anderson batted the lamp off the nightstand, plunging them into darkness, and then fumbled past the Gideon's Bible in the top drawer for his Smith & Wesson.

He could hear Ward clattering over the shattered glass to the window. The young agent was apparently dragging over his top mattress to use it as cover.

"Mind you don't get cut," Anderson whispered, wriggling into his shoes before moving in a crouch to the door. "See anything?"

"Give me a second."

"That was a shotgun. Twelve-gauge."

"I know," Ward said.

"Aimed high, just to scare us some."

"I'm getting movement out there."

Keeping his body behind the wall, Anderson cracked the door a few inches and peered out over his sights at the lawn separating their wing of the motel from the parking lot. His eyes were just beginning to adjust to the outside darkness when the night erupted into sulfurous fire that in a blink curled skyward into the shape of a huge cross. The flames threw plenty of light all around the motel courtyard, but no one was to be seen, as expected.

His revolver down at his side, Ward stepped over Anderson's legs and went out the door. The fire made his eyes seem even more fierce than usual.

Anderson joined him on the lawn. "Now you know what you're getting into, I suppose."

"I'm calling the inspector." Ward's voice sounded strange and wooden. "We're going to need more agents."

"For what?"

Ward lifted his chin at the cross, which was dripping fiery streams of fuel oil from the rag-wrapped cross beam.

"Would it make a difference if I told you that was exactly the wrong thing to do?"

"No," Ward said.

4

Television had turned it into Tut's tomb.

The house of the movie theater was dark and musty, and until an account could be set up with the electric company the only light was flowing in from the glass doors of the lobby. Anderson had taken one of a hundred and fifty empty seats. He was staring into the grayed-out silver screen, munching on a cheeseburger and slurping coffee from a Dixie cup.

"It's about time," Ward said after consulting his wristwatch. He was perched on the apron of the stage, tapping the scarred wainscoting with his heels. "You care to greet them with me?"

Anderson shook his head, then gestured with his burger toward the projection booth. "Movie's gonna start any minute."

"What do you think?" Ward asked, meaning the movie theater he'd rented as a command post. "Will it do?"

"Just dandy."

"Only seventy-five a month. It's private. Centrally located. Only windows are out front."

"And there's room for another fifty agents in the balcony. Just dandy, like I said." Anderson went back to eating, his eyes opaque in the gloom.

Sighing, Ward walked past Anderson, through the blackout curtains, and positioned himself in the lobby next to the ticket booth. He wanted to see the expressions on the faces of the townies when the parade hit Main Street. He wanted them to realize what the Federal Bureau of Integration could put together in less than twenty-four hours. And this wasn't all: unbeknownst to anyone in Mississippi except himself, the administrative wheels were being set into motion for the prompt establishment of a new field office in Jackson. Previously, responsibility for the state had been divided north and south between the Memphis and New Orleans offices. But now the Magnolia State was going to have its very own permanent nest of nigger-loving, communistic Hoover boys.

The shops and sidewalks looked so peaceful under the noon sun it was difficult to believe that this place had two faces, two hearts—one pleasant, gracious even; the other corrupt and unapologetically vicious. Anderson accepted the dichotomy because he was one of these people. But the affinity he had for them also compromised his effectiveness as an agent down here.

Yet Ward wasn't about to have him relieved. That would create bad blood between them which would last until one of them left the Bureau, and they might be made to work with each other in the future. Repeatedly.

No, Ward had been more subtle than that.

He had arranged for John Byrd to come down from Memphis with a team of agents handpicked from all over the Midwest. And twice that number was on standby should the situation here suddenly worsen. The Southern offices had not been drawn down in the event the troubles in Mississippi sparked a sympathetic reaction throughout the region.

Of John Byrd—he utterly lacked a personality, could think of nothing to say beyond shoptalk, and ate with his mouth open. But Byrd did precisely what he was told. Ward would leave Anderson in place here, nominally in the number two spot, but then channel all his operational orders through Byrd.

Even if Anderson figured out what was going on, Ward doubted that he would protest much. After all, he was being put on de facto holiday with full pay; he could mosey around town and talk the fine points of bream fishing and chitterlings cooking all he wanted.

Then, one by one, six black Dodge Polaras rounded the corner—all identical only because the Bureau had bought them at fleet price, but the locals didn't need to know that. The cars were uniform because they were part of the arsenal of a great, inexorable force that would descend on them if they refused to accept the inevitable.

Ward grinned.

The townies were freezing in their tracks, gaping at the convoy.

"Yeah," Ward whispered, "Reconstruction's back in town to stay, folks. Get used to it." And in that single word, he felt, the crux of the problem could be found: the Southern leadership, the same good old boys who'd ridden with Lee and Jackson and Beauregard, had finagled ways to derail Reconstruction before the Negro could be fully invested with his citizenship. As far as Ward was concerned, he and the FBI were down here on unfinished business from the last century.

The line of dark Dodges pulled up to the curb, and Ward stepped out to wave at Byrd, who as usual had the air of someone in immediate need of instructions.

"You want us to park here, Mr. Ward?" he asked, standing half out of his car.

"Yes, fine."

"What about our equipment? Want us to offload it out back later on?"

"No, bring it all through the front," Ward said, inclining his head toward the small, curious crowd that was assembling across the street. "And don't be afraid to show it off a little." He shook the hands of the agents, who then turned and began carrying their weapons and equipment inside the theater.

The townies seemed adequately impressed with the Remington Wingmaster shotguns, but they saved their loudest murmurings for the two Thompson submachine guns Ward had requested.

"Where are the mortars, Boss?" Anderson had wandered outside, looking amused as he nodded hellos to the agents.

"Can you operate one, Mr. Anderson?"

Anderson just chuckled, but quickly sobered as a showroom-new Oldsmobile convertible cruised past, flying small Confederate battle flags from the front fenders. The aquiline-faced driver ignored the agents as he continued serenely down the street. He double-parked in front of the Masonic Hall, got out, and warmly clasped a half-dozen hands in the course of promenading inside.

"Who do you suppose that cracker is?"

"No cracker. I'm a cracker, Boss. He's money."

"Klan maybe?"

"Klan absolutely," Anderson said.

"How do you know?"

"Wear a pointy hat long enough you get a pointy head."

"I'll run a registration check on the plates."

"You do that, Boss." Then Anderson loosened the knot of his tie and started down the sidewalk, keeping to the shade as he apparently window-shopped.

Ward watched him for a moment, then hurried back inside the theater.

Anderson sensed Ward watching him most of the way down the block. But when he turned at the corner to glance back, the young agent was no longer standing under the blank marquee.

"Probably thinks I'm out fucking the dog," he muttered to himself, then realized with a start that there might be womenfolk nearby. Fortunately, there was none, just a colored kid on a homemade scooter who probably hadn't heard him anyway over the rumble of his caster wheels on the cement.

Actually, Anderson felt he had something damned important to do: convince these people that the United States government was not on the verge of launching another war against them. As he had told Ward earlier today, the strongest argument the Klan had was that the feds were prepared to occupy Jackson and run Mississippi as a conquered territory as it had after the War Between the States. Bringing in all these agents was only adding fuel to that argument.

He stopped beside the hardware store window, his smile turning wistful as he inspected a colorful assortment of hand-tied flies, both wet and dry varieties, streamers too: Royal Coachman, Parmachene Belle, Gray Hackle, Quill Gordon, Mickey Finn, Light Tiger, and Black Ghost. Just the names themselves conjured a sensation of floating ease, of green water and blue sky. When was the last time he'd gone fishing? He couldn't recall.

Male laughter spilled out the open door of he barbershop, and Anderson found himself drifting toward the sound of it.

It had felt good to belong to a town like this, to be known and trusted, to be rooted to a piece of turf. But then he had gone out and done the very thing guaranteed to make him an outsider the rest of his days. Why? What things inside him had set him apart?

The laughter was cut short as he stepped inside.

"Afternoon, gentlemen."

Sheriff Stuckey, who'd been reading something from the paper to the others, grimaced, but only as long as it took him to paste on a congenial, somewhat sly expression. He was obviously still boiling under the surface for the way Ward had treated him. "Why, Mr. Anderson, have enough reinforcements now arrived so you can take the rest of the day off?"

He decided to ignore the comment.

On the ointment shelf behind the barber a radio was going. Ball game from St. Louis. The barber had lathered up a fat man for a shave, and two porcine eyes glared out of the smeared cream at him.

"Mr. Anderson," Stuckey went on, "say hello to our mayor, Lyle Tilman."

"Mr. Mayor."

The portly man moved a chewed cigar to the

other side of his mouth with a roll of his lips. "Pleased to make your acquaintance, Mr. Anderson."

Easing into the waiting chair with least amount of Scotch-tape repair work to its burgundy-colored vinyl, Anderson took in the shop, inhaled its odors of bay rum and hot clipper oil. Above the barber's license hung a white-tail buck with dusty antlers and even dustier eyes. A semi-nude coquette beamed at him from a Vargas calendar that just as convincingly could have been dated 1924 instead of 1964. Tucked in the frame of the long mirror were yellowed newspaper clippings about local fishing and hunting records.

"You care for a trim this morning?" the barber asked.

"No, thank you," Anderson drawled, easing into the phlegmatic speech patterns of the others as he ran his hand over his balding pate, "I got me a deal with a barber who only charges by the square inch."

The men chuckled, politely.

"Where you originally from, Mr. Anderson?" Mayor Tilman asked.

"North of here."

"How far north?" The piggish eyes were hard on him.

"I was born on the mannerly side of the Tallahatchie."

More chuckling. But the mayor's point hadn't been lost on Anderson.

"A Hill boy, then," Tilman observed.

"That's right, sir."

"Then you must have some idea how we all feel down here."

"With your hands?"

No laughter followed this, but Anderson hadn't

expected any: his own tone of voice had been humorless. He was already fed up with the good-old-boy insinuations Tilman was flinging at him like corn pone batter off a spatula. The first was that he was a scalawag, a Southern white who'd opposed secession and then sided with the Yankee carpetbaggers. The second was that he was a stuck-up Hill Mississippian who had only a vague, twisted notion what Delta folk were all about. And there was yet another: that he was imposing on their graciousness.

"We feel, Mr. Anderson, that it's improper for outsiders to tell us how to live our lives. Particular for those who have little understanding and even less affection for us."

"Do you count me among those outsiders?" Anderson asked, still smiling.

"Not at all, sir. But you more than they should realize our nigras were contented till these beatnik collegiates descended on us like locusts to stir up discontent were there was none before."

"None, Mr. Mayor?"

"That is fundamentally correct, sir."

Anderson turned to Stuckey, who'd tightly rolled up his newspaper and was holding it as if it were a snake whose neck he intended to snap. "Well, gentlemen, your colored must be different from them I was raised around."

"Could be," Stuckey said. "But the mayor's point is that nobody complained."

"Nobody dared. We both know that, Sheriff."

"Do we?"

"Sure, and I'm not saying what's wrong or right. I'm just talking about what is. Hell, Sheriff, I did your job for eight years. Down here, we got two standards of law enforcement, one for white and one for colored. Is that so hard to admit? Hah, we Southerners tell the whole world with pride we got ourselves two separate and distinct shows going on down here. A two-ring circus with the good Lord's stamp of approval on it."

"Separate but equal, Mr. Anderson," Mayor Tilman noted, "If I might particularize."

Anderson grinned. "Like I said, I'm just talking about what is."

"This is a law-abiding community," Stuckey said, his voice suddenly a pitch higher. "That's what *is*."

"I don't doubt that for a minute, Sheriff."

"Seems to me you doubt plenty for somebody calling hisself a Southerner."

Anderson fell silent. Stuckey, in his spurt of temper, had hit upon something. Doubt—is that why he had left Mississippi so many years ago? Whatever this unhappy thing was, it had been with him as long as he could remember. It had spread its claws inside him the first time he stared up at a Confederate statue, like the one now glinting greenly across the square, and felt that swelling of fierce, defiant pride being adulterated by something else, something indefinable but nettlesome, something that suggested the image of a poisoned mule bloating in a field.

The special agent's momentary quiet had persuaded the sheriff to turn affable again: "For chrissakes, Anderson, we both know this whole situation's like three sticks of old dynamite—"

"That's it, Ray," Mayor Tilman chimed in, "time has slowly crystallized this situation so it can't take rough handling."

"Shake it up and we'll be scraping folks off the street with a flat-nose shovel."

Still seated, Anderson took a languid stretch.

"I'm just down here looking for three missing kids, asking a couple questions."

"And if all this was boiled down to gravy there wouldn't be much to it," the mayor said. "These kids you're hunting for are probably back there in New York City, laughing at all the commotion they've stirred up."

"Well, let's sure hope so."

"What's with your boss man anyhow?" Tilman asked.

"Mr. Hoover?"

"The selfsame. We had nothing but a most profound respect for J. Edgar before this business."

"Relied on him for damn near all our training," Stuckey said.

"He can use some serious talking to, Mr. Anderson."

"How's that, Mr. Mayor?"

"Well, it's evident some wrong ideas about the South got into his head—everybody running around raggedy-assed, backward and illiterate, eating sow belly and fried okra three times a day."

"So what would you all have me tell Mr. Hoover? It'd have to be brief. He don't have much time for special agents."

"In a nutshell, now?" Mayor Tilman paused while the barber's blade scraped under his nose. "I'd acquaint him with the simple fact you already lit upon, Mr. Anderson—we got ourselves two cultures down here. One white. One nigra. And that's how it's gonna stay."

"Amen," Stuckey said.

"Don't you agree, Mr. Anderson?" the mayor asked, somewhat insistently.

The special agent had come to his feet and turned to the barber, who'd obviously been paying more attention to the game than the conversation. "What's the score?"

"St. Louis on top. Five—nothing."

"What inning?"

"Bottom of the seventh."

"You play baseball in high school, Mr. Anderson?" the mayor asked, ever the politician grubbing for common ground.

"Varsity all four years. But it was a small school."

"A fine and spirited game, what?"

"You bet. Only one where a colored man can wave a stick at a white man without starting a riot." When they didn't laugh, Anderson said, "Afternoon, gentlemen."

Outside on the hot sidewalk again, it occurred to him that no one had brought up the ruckus at the motel last night to him, just as long ago no one had mentioned Monroe's mule to his daddy.

"Welcome home, Roop," he muttered to himself.

John Byrd found Ward pacing and thinking up in the relative privacy of the mezzanine. "Mr. Ward?" he asked, waving a sheet torn from a steno pad.

"Yeah, John?"

"Return on your plate, sir."

"From Motor Vehicles in Jackson?"

"No," Byrd admitted, "they're still insisting there's no record on file and are—"

"Asking us to reconfirm the number. Right." Shaking his head, Ward accepted the paper. "From now on, run anything we need through our Memphis office. They can relay the request through the Tennessee state police so Jackson doesn't know it's us asking for it."

"Very good, sir."

Ward's eyes widened as he read Byrd's neat block printing.

"Is that the Clayton Townley I think it is, sir?"

"The one and only, John. Same Tupelo address." Ward found himself grinning: he was gratified that the Grand Wizard of the White Knights of the Ku Klux Klan had decided to drive over a hundred miles in his brand new Oldsmobile convertible to find out what the FBI was really doing in Delta country. That meant Ward's efforts had touched a nerve, and in this business it was often the only milestone indicating some progress was being made.

Byrd looked like he was sitting on something else.

"What is it, John?"

"Well, a funny call just came in no sooner than we got the phone installed . . ."

"And?"

"Anonymous informant says he wants to meet with us at seven tonight. Says he knows where a station wagon with New Jersey plates has been dumped."

Ward's pulse had quickened. "Where does he want to meet?"

"Intersection of the state highway and county road ten miles south of town." Byrd began rubbing his forehead—his sign that something was worrying him, Ward had learned.

"Did it sound like a setup to you?"

"Yes . . . no." Byrd gave a sheepish smile. "I don't know, sir. He had a funny accent."

"Funny?"

"Yeah, not white, but not Negro either. Like nothing I've heard before."

"Cajun maybe?"

"No, sir."

Ward wondered if Anderson might be able to explain this, but then rebuked himself for even thinking of turning to the apathetic agent again—for any reason.

Anderson ventured inside the beauty parlor if only because of the mingled perfumes that were drifting out the open door onto the sidewalk. Somehow this made him recall how fondly he liked the company of women, especially after listening to a bunch of men ballyhoo about their convictions and the right way to run the world.

The interior looked like the most industrious place in town, although like the barbershop it fell silent as soon as he stepped inside—except for the whining of the big hair dryers that looked like astronaut helmets. Only one of these noisy devices in a long line of them was vacant, so Anderson sat there, crossed his legs, and assumed a silly grin while he waited for someone to do something about his presence.

It was much more fun to josh with women. They intuited right off what you were after deep down, and usually they didn't mind as long as you furnished them with a couple of laughs along the way. Men had so many more reasons to be suspicious.

A pretty little thing of perhaps nineteen with plump cheeks and platinum-colored hair was first to take the bait. "Can I help you?"

Anderson primped the scraggly gray hair that seemed to sprout on the back of his neck two hours after he had a haircut. "I hate the way I look."

"Oh?" She was already close to the giggles and had to bite her underlip.

"What do you think about a permanent wave? Or a bleach? Yours looks pretty." He lowered his voice. "Did you get yours done here?"

"No," she whispered back, "in Jackson."

A woman his age with a pronounced overbite twisted around under her dryer to have a look at his head. "I think a wig's your only hope, hon. You ain't gonna be able to do much with that cue ball. Connie," she said to the girl, "toss this gentleman a towel so he can comb his hair."

All the women shrieked.

Anderson laughed with them, although he was also blushing slightly. He had not liked losing his hair; girls had always commented that he had nice hair, and before the war he'd even worn it with a big wave at the front.

"You look like you just swallowed the canary," the woman went on, gently patting his arm to assure him that no harm had been intended. Southern women were born wary of a man's ego, and maybe slightly contemptuous of it, too.

"Does it show that bad?"

"Most assuredly does, hon. But if you come to town to ask some questions, this is the only place to do it. You'll hear all you care, maybe even some you don't."

"I was just wondering," Anderson said, pointing out through the venetian blinds and disregarding the pink blur that had just passed in front of him, "who owns that chrome showboat."

"His name's Clayton Townley," a new voice said softly. It came from a pink-uniformed woman who'd just crossed from the back to the sink nearest the window. She was carding some jet black hair out of a brush with a comb. Her hands were somewhat chafed.

Anderson nodded his thanks to her, and she looked away with a vague smile. He had last seen her arguing on the sidewalk with Deputy Pell.

"Nice car," he said, afraid that if he said nothing she would slip away again into the back room where she had obviously been—for he'd looked around for her first thing upon coming inside.

"I guess."

He liked the fact that she didn't seem impressed by Clayton Townley's car, or perhaps even by Townley himself. He also wondered how Special Agent-in-Charge Ward would take the news that the grand wizard was here in the glorious flesh. He'd probably throw down the gauntlet and challenge Townley to a joust on Main Street.

"Are you one of them FBI gentlemen?" the woman with the overbite asked.

"Yes, ma'am."

"But you talk"—her eyes darted in search of the right word—"normal."

"Yes, well, that's a long story—and I'm just here for a tint and a perm."

She lightly touched his forearm again. "If you ask me, I think it's a shame if'n those two kids are dead. But I sure hope you find them."

"Actually, there's three kids missing. A colored kid too."

"I know that."

"But you just said two, ma'am."

The woman at the sink then asked, "Do you honestly think you people'd be down here like you are if it wasn't for the two white boys?"

Anderson stared up at the whirring ceiling fan with a lopsided grin. "No. Maybe not, miss—"

"That's missus to you, sir," Connie said, sweep-

ing past with shampoo bubbles all over her hands.
"Mrs. Clinton Pell. But *I'm* single."

Mrs. Pell avoided his stare as she lit up a smoke,
took a few hungry inhalations, then rested it on
the lip of the sink while she finished cleaning up
the brush. He realized that he had known all
along that she was Pell's wife, but just hadn't wanted
to admit it. It was strange: how he felt more sorry
for himself about this than he did for her. Whatever, the story of the marriage was in the corners
of her eyes and in her hands. But there was no
use in feeling superior to Pell; he hadn't done
much better for a woman no less lovely. "How
long have you—"

"Constance Faye," Mrs. Pell said sharply, interrupting him, "again . . . please don't stroll around
with your hands dripping like that."

"Yes, ma'am." But Connie didn't sound very
contrite, and she went on dripping bubbles onto
the marbled green and black linoleum.

"What'd you say, sir?" Mrs. Pell asked disinter-
estedly.

"Nothing important," he said, for his eyes were
now fixed on an old GMC pickup that had stopped
at the intersection in front of the shop but not
moved on immediately. He had the impression
that there were three men inside the cab and that
the fellow on the far side of the truck was either
drunk or sick.

Suddenly the pickup sped forward. Anderson
tracked it for a few seconds, noting that it had no
rear license plate, before his gaze swept back to
the crosswalk. A Negro was lying in it, a battered,
bloody youth with his arms folded across his chest
as if he were lying in repose at a funeral parlor.

5

"It's Hollis Johnson," Anderson told Ward, who had just jogged down the street from the theater with an ungainly John Byrd attempting to keep up with him. "The colored kid you had breakfast with."

At first Ward thought that the young Negro was dead, he was lying so still and looked so badly beaten. But then Hollis groaned. He draped the crook of his arm over his swollen eyes—the sun had been glaring into them—and tried to lift his head off the hot pavement.

"You stay right down there for a minute, boy," Sheriff Stuckey said.

"I gots to—"

"Lay still like I say, boy, till we see if anything's broke."

"Nothing broke," Hollis went on, his voice a delirious rasp.

"Something sure bit you to beat all hell."

"Dogs. The dogs what was guarding me in the bale dump."

"Where was this?" Anderson asked, leaning down.

"Okay now, Hoover boys," Stuckey said before Hollis could answer, "we'll handle this. Local problem." He turned toward Pell, who'd materialized in a patrol car within seconds after the throng had gathered around the prostrate man: "Clinton."

"Yeah, Sheriff." He jumped off the fender of his cruiser, on which he'd been lounging, champing on a toothpick, and strolled over. His shadow fell across Hollis's face, but then he moved aside a step so the young man was blinking into the sun again.

"This don't look good," Stuckey said confidentially. "What if TV news had been out and about?"

"I don't see any cameras, sir."

"I know that. I was just saying 'what if.' " Stuckey raised his voice again: "Now I want you to look into this, because this just won't do, now, Deputy. This just won't do."

"All right, sir."

Ward caught Anderson smirking at this exchange.

The sheriff must have also caught the agent's look, for he said, "I thought I already asked you Hoover boys to leave us to our business."

"On our way, Sheriff," Anderson said, wheeling to go.

Stuckey's tone of voice had been enough to make Ward want to linger a few moments more, but Anderson caught him at the elbow and led him back toward the theater. "Let's do like the man asks, Boss." A moment later, after making sure Byrd was out of earshot, he added: "And maybe you'll think twice next time before you go talking to a colored man in front of a white audience."

"Hold it there." Ward pulled his arm out of Anderson's grasp. "Are you suggesting I caused this?"

"Well, you try to buddy up to this boy, and next

thing he's laying beaten and bit in the middle of Main Street. I highly suspect some connection."

"The connection to be made," Ward said, walking again, "is with Clayton Townley's arrival."

"What does the grand wizard have to do with the price of cotton?"

"Everything."

"You're losing me, Boss."

"Dammit, this was just a show for his sake."

Anderson chuckled. "Folks here don't have to prove a thing to Clayton Townley. And the good old boys who did this—well, they just wanted to make sure no colored talk to us."

"Sorry, I don't buy that," Ward said, even though he did buy it to a certain degree—for the first thing he'd felt upon running up to Hollis Johnson was a bewildering but smarting guilt that his eagerness to help had somehow harmed an innocent man instead. Suddenly it seemed in harmony with convoluted ways of Mississippi that his intentions had been so crudely subverted.

Anderson was probably right: he had triggered the beating by violating the Jim Crow section of the diner. But he would do it again and then again until there were no such sections in restaurants and bus stations. Anderson had to understand that. When he finally did, then Alan Ward would feel better about confessing his own lapses into uncertainty.

Anderson was included in the evening's operation only at the last minute. Up until that time, Ward had been more than willing to leave the agent to a leisurely dinner and his pint of Jim Beam sour mash. But just as the tactical team was on its way out the front doors of the theater, the phone rang. Ward picked it up. It was the anonymous informant, beating around the bush but evidently calling for no other reason than to confirm that the G-men were definitely coming to the rendezvous. Ward cared for neither the apparent purpose of the call nor the man's breathy voice and indefinable accent. So, stifling his reluctance, he had gone back into the theater to fetch Anderson, who was sitting with his shoes propped on the seat in front of him and sucking on a lime Popsicle. "I've changed my mind, Mr. Anderson. I'd like you to come along." Thank God the agent had said nothing and simply followed him up the aisle, out the lobby, and into the leading car of the small convoy. Ward would not have been able to contain himself had Anderson tried to get a dig or two in.

In the course of the afternoon planning session with Byrd, he had decided on using three cars and five agents, six now with the inclusion of Anderson.

The lead car would hold Byrd, Anderson, and himself, but it would not be the first to approach the intersection of the state and county highways ten miles south of town. A white Ford Falcon with Mississippi plates, rented from a dealership in Jackson, would be driven past the site by Brodsky, the agent who, with the face of a Manhattan cabdriver, looked the least like a G-man. Lacking a radio, he would signal with his tail lamps if everything looked all right to him—or double back on foot through the woods and fields with a Thompson to present the bushwhackers with a little surprise if the meeting proved to be a setup.

The final car, the fastest of the Dodge Polaras,

would carry the two agents serving as backup to the operation. They would hang back until needed.

All in all, Ward believed it to be a flexible plan that minimized the danger to the agents as much as it could ever be. There was always some residual risk. The name of the game, he reminded himself—but none too blithely. His healed gunshot wound was vaguely throbbing.

As soon as Byrd was behind the wheel and Ward situated on the other end of the front seat, Anderson said from the back while chewing on the Popsicle stick, "Might want to pull out of town one by one."

"Why's that?"

"Don't want to look like a Mardi Gras parade, do we?"

"Mardi Gras?" Byrd echoed uncomprehendingly.

"We might leave town by different streets too," Anderson went on. "Link up a ways south of here."

Ward almost choked on his own words: "Good point, Mr. Anderson."

"Thank you."

"Hang on a minute, John, while I tell the others."

"Yes, sir."

Ward damned himself for not having thought of this as he passed the word to the other cars. By the time he got back to the lead car, Anderson was snoozing, or maybe only pretending to nap. Either way, he didn't open his eyes again until they met up with the other cars again three miles south of town. The descending sun was low enough to throw its orange light through the window on Anderson's side, and the man roused himself with a wide, smiling yawn. "Morning, boys," he said cheerfully.

The shotgun Ward had jammed earlier up

against the seat was vibrating down against his heels. He pushed it back again. "Do you think they have the nerve to hit us?" he asked Anderson.

"Oh, they got the nerve. What's unknown is whether or not they got the reason."

Ward hesitated, but then asked anyway, "What's your gut feeling about this?"

"Don't have one. Seldom do about anything. I learned one thing from the United States Army—just sit tight and see what pops up."

Brodsky passed them in the Falcon, giving a thumbs-up as he assumed the lead.

Ward checked the rearview mirror and saw that the backup car was beginning to fade into the distance.

"Six miles from town, sir," Byrd said.

Ward prayed that his slight nervousness wasn't apparent to Anderson and Byrd. He was recalling what it had felt like to get shot—the hammer blow that had spun him around like a toy top, and ten minutes later the relentless ache that had suddenly undulated up out of the numbness and lasted for months, defying even the most potent painkillers and putting his return to duty in question. In order to restore strength to his shattered shoulder, he had done countless chin-ups and push-ups. The first few had been nearly made him faint. But he had gritted his teeth and counted them out, all because nothing was going to stop him from going South again. That bullet wasn't going to win.

"Eight miles, sir," Byrd said, his hands a bit tighter on the wheel.

Even Anderson was sitting up.

Brodsky's Falcon was little more than a white dot where the highway narrowed to infinity.

"He should be at the crossroads about now."

"Pick it up some, John."

Byrd applied more toe to the accelerator pedal.

Anderson braced his forearms against the back of the front seat and peered over Ward's shoulder. "How well do you know Brodsky, Boss?"

"Fairly well."

"Does he know what he sees when he sees it?"

"He gets the job done."

Anderson didn't seem satisfied, but he sat back again.

Ward asked himself, what was he supposed to say? That Brodsky was infallible?

"Nine miles, Mr. Ward."

"Come on, taillights," he muttered, watching the Falcon continue past the intersection with the county road. "Come on, Brod."

"Want me to slow down again, sir?"

While Ward pondered this, Anderson said, "You might, Byrd. Never be in a rush to meet trouble. And avoid it altogether what if you can."

"Mr. Ward?"

He was going to get shot again. A heavy, enervating feeling was flowing over him. "Do as Anderson suggests."

Then the Falcon's red lamps flashed three times, and Ward let go of the breath he'd been holding. "Continue, John." He got on the radio and informed the backup unit that all appeared to be well at the crossroads. He did so briefly, for the Bureau had no radio repeater in southwest Mississippi, and he was fudging by using one of the frequencies assigned to the state's Highway Safety Patrol. The last thing he wanted was troopers sniffing around while he attempted to recover the vehicle.

"That's just Brodsky's opinion," Anderson said when Ward had hung the microphone out of sight again.

"How's that, Mr. Anderson?"

"It's just his opinion that everything's all right. I think we oughta reserve our own judgment."

At the crossroads stood a small gas station with a white kid sitting just outside the office door on an upturned soft-drink crate. He seemed unconcerned by anything, even the black Dodge as it slowly pulled onto the oiled sand of the lot.

"Dodge hasn't turned out anything bullet-proof since 1945," Anderson said, getting out even before Byrd had come to a complete stop. He casually rested his hand within inches of his concealed, holstered revolver. Waving to the kid, whose insouciance was a good sign, he ambled toward the detached cinder-block restrooms. He covered Ward and Byrd from that flank as they cautiously left the car. Byrd had parked it on the asphalt pad between the two pump islands.

Anderson smelled tobacco smoke drifting out of the transom over the door marked MEN.

Drawing his Smith & Wesson, he approached the door as quietly as he could. Then he kicked it open.

The man within didn't flinch. He continued to lean against the beaverboard partition masking the toilet, arms crossed over his chest, his eyes bright on Anderson's handgun. He wore baggy khaki trousers and a sleeveless T-shirt that hadn't been washed anytime recently.

"Evening, Chief," Anderson said, patting him down for an ankle holster. He was clean. "You alone?"

The man nodded, the tips of his greasy black braids jiggling.

As Anderson put away his revolver, he could hear Byrd and Ward trotting up to the restroom door. "Mr. Byrd," he said without taking his eyes off the copper-complected man standing before him, "how about us not bunching up—and you keeping watch outside?"

"Very well, Mr. Anderson."

"What's your name?" Ward demanded of the man.

"Don't matter, mister," he said, almost in a whisper. "Names don't have to matter none in this."

Ward asked Anderson, "What kind of accent is that? It sounds a little French."

Anderson grinned, and then the man did too as he took a puff of his cigarette. "Muskhogean, I suppose. But you may be right about the French. His people teamed up with the Frenchies when New Orleans was still theirs."

"What?"

It was nice to see Special Agent-in-Charge Ward looking unsure of himself for once. "Unless I'm wrong, our friend here is Choctaw."

Again the Indian confirmed Anderson's words with a nod.

"Most his people were carted off to Oklahoma with the four other civilized tribes. But some Choctaw folks didn't feel like being carted off." Anderson lifted his chin at the Choctaw: "It's a mite close in here, Chief. Care to talk outside?"

"With you," he said, obviously meaning that he wanted to exclude Ward and Byrd from the conversation.

"Whatever you want." On the way out, Anderson noticed the Indian's inch-long fingernails.

* * *

Ward sat beside Byrd in the Dodge, both front doors wide open to allow the humid breeze to pass over their sweaty faces. Anderson was still jawing with the Choctaw out in a clutch of rusted fifty-gallon drums behind the station, and the other two FBI cars were parked a few hundred yards down the state highway.

"What do you think, Mr. Ward?"

He could only shrug; he wasn't sure what he thought. Why was Anderson taking such a long time interviewing the Indian?—unless he was increasingly suspicious that the sighting of the station wagon was bogus, sucker bait for an elaborate setup.

All Ward knew was that he had a sour stomach, and he was far too young for the stomach problems he'd been having of late.

At last Anderson turned and shambled back toward the Polara, leaving the Indian to ease down onto the lid of one of the metal drums.

"Well, Boss," he said, squatting down on knees that cracked and sitting on his heels, "he's sticking to his story about a Ford wagon ditched out in the swamp."

"How far from here?"

"Six, seven miles into the reservation."

Ward checked the shadows—the sun was already gone behind the pines to the west. He figured they had less than an hour of usable light remaining, and he didn't relish the thought of being led into a swamp just as night fell.

Anderson might have read the concern in his face, for he said, "Yeah, it'll be black as tar soon. And I don't know these people from Adam. A few

Choctaw where I come from up north, but not many."

"Are they trustworthy?" Ward asked, immediately feeling naive when Anderson laughed.

"Hell, what's trustworthy? Given the choice, they'll look after themselves—like damn near everybody else in this world. But as far as natural meanness, I'd put my money on a Chickasaw over a Choctaw any day of the week."

"Excuse me, Mr. Anderson," Byrd asked, "but why did he contact us instead of the sheriff?"

"Same question occurred to me, Mr. Byrd." Anderson gave a casual glance back toward the Choctaw, who'd lit another cigarette but hadn't moved from the drum. "He said he don't care much for Ray Stuckey. He wouldn't elaborate, but I figure any bad blood there is must stem from an old collar. These folks take an arrest kinda personal. Worse thing you can do to a Choctaw or a Chickasaw is shut him up out of the sunlight. Years ago, when I ran my own jail, I had one go crazy on me. Had to pack him off to the state mental hospital."

"What's this guy want?" Ward asked, sounding more cynical than he'd intended. "Money?"

"I don't think so, but he'd take it if we offered." Anderson spat between his knees—Mississippi was apparently reawakening old habits. Ward looked away. "No, Boss, cash isn't the reason he phoned. He's probably the local holy man—I remember hearing somewheres the priests grow their nails long. He wants to be rid of the wagon."

"What do you mean?"

"He wants the Ford dragged out of the swamp and towed off the reservation."

"But why?"

"Well, he won't come out and say, but I suppose he thinks it's bad medicine or something."

Ward and Byrd exchanged a glance. "Does this guy know more than what he's saying, Mr. Anderson?"

Again the agent laughed. "Don't we all, Boss?"

"I'm asking you a serious question."

Anderson's eyes hardened a little. "And I'm giving you a serious answer. The decision is yours—do we go out there tonight with this man or not?"

Rubbing his forefinger over his lower lip, Ward stared off at the Indian again. If he allowed this tactical team to be led into an ambush and one or more agents died, his career was down the toilet—and with it would go his ambition of someday heading up one of the Bureau's major offices, like New York or Chicago. Yet, on the other hand, if he delayed until morning and in the intervening hours, the suspects destroyed any evidentiary value the Ford station wagon might still hold, he would most likely be pulled off this assignment.

Anderson was smiling at him.

That was enough to make Ward say, "Let's do it."

"Whatever you say, Boss." Anderson rose and went after the Choctaw.

Ward reached for the microphone and tersely instructed the backup car to join up with him, but before doing so to tell Brodsky to return to town in the Falcon and inform Memphis by telephone that the team was proceeding onto the Choctaw reservation. If worse came to worst, he didn't want the Bureau to spend days, even weeks, searching a quarter of Mississippi for them.

Anderson got in through the back door on Byrd's

side of the Dodge. Following standard procedure for once, he would protect the driver in the event the Choctaw proved unfriendly. Early in his career Ward had been kicked in the head by a prisoner who'd been seated directly behind him— and nearly crashed his car into a highway guardrail. Silently the Choctaw entered on the side opposite from Anderson. He smelled of woodsmoke and perspiration.

The backup car pulled in behind, the two agents stone-faced.

"Where to, Chief?" Anderson asked.

"South . . . first road going right."

Byrd drove away from the gas station and checked the rearview mirror, as if assuring himself that the backup unit was still there.

Hugged by thick undergrowth, the side road soon turned to mud, and Ward became concerned that the vehicles would become mired. But he had made his decision. Besides, there was no place for the two Dodges to turn around. "How far now?" he asked the Indian.

"A ways."

Small maize fields began to break up the brushy, stunted woods. The golden tassels seemed to glow through the fading light as if they were aflame.

"We going to be able to winch this wagon out of the water?" Anderson asked.

The Choctaw smirked. "It's gonna be a job. I guarantee it."

Ahead, bluish smoke was sifting across the road.

Byrd leaned over the steering wheel. "What's that from?"

"Village," the Indian said. "Keep going."

The two cars crept through a collection of shanties fashioned from corrugated tin, canvas, and billboard plywood. A few of the dwellings had thatched roofs, probably a holdover from native days. Beside one, a pre-war pickup stood on blocks, and vines twined up through the hoodless engine compartment. Despite the smoldering fire pits, no one was visible.

"Where is everybody?" Anderson asked.

For once, the Choctaw didn't answer.

Beyond the village the countryside gently fell away toward some lowlands which were already a deep purple with night.

Byrd asked if he should turn on his headlamps, but Ward said no.

The road, growing even muddier and narrower, was crowded by young palmettos—an impenetrable wall of spiky green, and then these gave way to a shadowy cypress stand. Beards of Spanish moss dangled limply for there was no breeze down here.

Ward turned to examine the Indian's face. He was expressionless. Anderson was smiling, but his hand was also inside his coat.

"How did you find the car?" Ward asked the Choctaw, if only to break the man's unsettling quiet.

"Hunting."

"What were you hunting?"

He yawned, a front tooth was missing. "Anything."

"What about other roads leading down here? Are there any?"

"A couple."

"But the best one goes through your village, right?"

"I guess."

"Did you see the station wagon being driven through your village?"

"I found it hunting," the Indian insisted, his dark eyes flaring for an instant.

Ward turned around again as Byrd suddenly hit the brakes. "I can't make out the road anymore, Mr. Ward."

"Where does it go from here, Chief?" Anderson asked.

"No place. This is it." He got out, and the others did the same, although more cautiously. The shutting of the car doors echoed in the cypresses, briefly punctuating the menacing hum of insects that heretofore had been covered by the engine noise.

Ward directed his flashlight beam out into the swamp. "Look at all the scum," he said quietly.

"Duckweed," Anderson corrected him, then became the first to fall in behind the Choctaw, who was following two badly rain-eroded tire-track impressions down into the water. Ward could find no shoe impressions, not after a week in country this rainy.

They rounded a cypress of enormous girth and there it was: a 1959 Ford Country Squire station wagon, sloping grill-first down into the stagnant waters. Half of the rear license plate was legible above the duckweed.

New Jersey, it read, the Garden State.

He was woken out of his doze by his dog.

His dog occasionally barked in the stillness of the night, but it most often proved to be nothing of concern. A corner of the old church creaking as it settled into the soggy ground on which it had been built. A possum waddling across the graveyard. Another dog on the prowl, sniffing at the back door for companionship. But the unaccustomed sharpness of this particular bark made the caretaker rise from his cot and reach for his eyeglasses.

His small room was only a few steps from the chancel, and he paused beside the pulpit. He peered out across the darkened pews, which in the dimness resembled the waves of the gulf.

Nothing.

"What you fussing for?" he asked the dog, who was cowering around his slippers.

Then from above came the tinkle of broken glass, and something like a firefly fluttered down into the center aisle, only to mushroom into a great blossom of flame. Feeding on the varnish of the recently refurbished pews, it soon filled the nave with a terribly crackling.

So fierce was the heat he threw his right arm across his eyes and stumbled back through the chancel door, tripping over his whimpering dog into the hallway.

A hand seized him by the neck of his terry-cloth robe and dragged him to his feet.

"You all right, boy?" a white voice demanded.

"Yes, suh," the caretaker croaked, thinking perhaps that he was one of the firemen from town. But then again, how had the fire department made it all the way out here when the blaze had just started? "I'm fine," he heard himself saying, sounding more scared than he felt.

"Well, that won't do."

"Suh?"

"You're not none of them voters, are you?"

"No, suh." The fire was roaring behind him, and a choking smoke was reaching into the hallway. The white man raised his hand—there seemed to be something in his hand. "Sorry, boy, but I got more of these to do tonight, and it won't do to have you running for help." And then these words shredded apart into a lightless silence.

6

The whippoorwills were going wild among the high branches of the cypresses, making whispery noises as they chased after enough insects to fill their bellies before dawn. From this Anderson concluded that the night was about over, a night that had passed with a lot of mosquito-bitten waiting and then cussing and a clutch that had burned out before the job was half done.

He even believed that the eastern sky was graying, although the emergency light atop the cab of the second tow truck—the first had limped back to town in first gear—was throwing red spangles all around the swamp and making it hard to pick out any subtle indications of morning.

Anderson found himself squinting because of the emergency light, and he shouted across the wallow churned up by the tires of the first truck, "Hey, Boss! Does the tow driver really need that bubblegum machine going?!"

A haggard-looking Ward turned to Byrd, who then trotted over to the truck, his shoes making sucking sounds in the mud, and told the kid driver to kill the red flasher.

His hands in his pockets, Ward crossed the wallow, stepping carefully over the half-inch cable the driver had attached to the rear chassis of the Ford station wagon—accomplishing this only because he had swung by his house to pick up the waders he used for duck hunting. Anderson had called out to the youth as he fumbled around in the putrid waters for something solid to hook up, "See anything inside, son?" He had stared for a long time through the tailgate window, then shook his head.

"This should have been finished hours ago," Ward now fumed, uncapping a stick of Chapstick and rubbing the stuff over his tight lips.

"Welcome to Mississippi," Anderson muttered.

The driver began backing up, his winch motor whining and his oversized rear tires slipping enough to flail up a shower of mud that caught Byrd unawares, splattering him.

Anderson smiled.

But as the cable went taut, he suggested to Ward that they step around to the far side of the handiest tree should it suddenly snap: "Nothing gets throwed away down here, Boss. That cable's probably left over from the Confederate naval defenses at Mobile."

Ward didn't laugh, but as he joined Anderson in a withdrawal of several yards he looked as if the joking words had suggested an idea to him. Addressing him as "boss" no longer produced the desired effect. In fact, Ward seemed to be accepting it as his due, so Anderson was considering dropping the bit in favor of some new irritant.

The tow truck began drifting to the side—and the station wagon wasn't budging.

"Son of a bitch," Ward said.

"Lucky that old Choctaw boy found it when he

did. Another week and it'd have been sunk in up to the roof." Suddenly thinking of the Indian, Anderson looked around for him, but shortly after the arrival of the first truck he had vanished without a word of farewell.

The driver eased off the accelerator and got out, slamming the cab door behind him. Previously he had cut some brush with a machete he kept behind the seat and now spread some of the branches in the muck behind the rear tires.

Then he climbed up and tried again.

"How far is Mobile from here?" Ward abruptly asked.

"I don't know—eighty, a hundred miles."

"Any Navy facilities there?"

"Sure. But there's a naval air station a helluva lot closer than that."

"Where?"

"Near Meridian."

Ward sank back into his thoughts again, and Anderson felt too weary to ask him what masterstroke he was dreaming up.

Then came a wrenching groan as the swamp bottom gave up the station wagon.

"All right," Byrd said, clapping.

The landed Ford was leaking water from its door seams. Ward stepped up and sprang the latch on the driver's side. The door flew open, forcefully enough to jam the agent's fingers—which he then shook—and a flood of turbid green water gushed out.

Anderson approached the vehicle from the passenger side. As the water quickly receded, he kept expecting at least one swollen, albino-looking corpse to appear along the floorboards. And when Ward suddenly gave a cry he thought one had been found.

"Body?" he asked.

"No," Ward said, scampering back on his heels and looking at something in the mud. "Snake."

"What kind?"

"Don't know . . . but it's wiggling away."

"They tend to do that if you stand up to them." Fishing his flashlight out of his jacket pocket, Anderson ran the beam over the soggy interior of the station wagon. No victims. The hunt would go on.

Ward slowly came around the hood and asked a little gruffly, as if trying to recover some dignity after being frightened by the snake, "What do you think now? Are they fucking off up North, laughing, like Stuckey says?"

"No, they're down here someplace."

"Alive, then?"

"No," Anderson said quietly. "They're dead."

"I agree."

Anderson pointed at the heat-faded paint of the dashboard and the melted spot on the vinyl headliner directly above. "Somebody tried to torch it in a half-assed kinda way."

"Why didn't he finish the job?"

"Hell, I don't know. Maybe he felt the clock breathing down his neck. Or realized all of a sudden that the Choctaw might see the fire and come running. I just don't know." Kneeling, using the blade of his hand, Anderson carefully wiped some of the duckweed off the floormat: it was burned, as was the underlying carpet where the accelerant, most likely gasoline, had seeped. The long period of submersion would complicate the identification of the flammable liquid, but that was the lab boy's problem.

Ward had removed the registration card from the visor holder. "This is definitely it," he said after a moment. "Belongs to our New Jersey victim's parents."

Rising, Anderson left the station wagon to the other agents and strolled over to the edge of the swamp. The rising light was beginning to reveal how truly vast these wetlands were, for the surface of the water was turning silver. He wanted a cigarette badly, but promised himself that he wouldn't beg one off Special Agent Macmillan, who'd been chain-smoking ever since they'd arrived here yesterday evening. One Old Gold this morning and he'd be back to three packs a day by nightfall.

He turned on sopping footfalls nearing him from behind. It was Ward, looking reflective as he scratched a big mosquito welt on his forehead.

The young agent stood silently beside Anderson for several seconds, gazing out across the swamp, before finally asking, "How deep out there?"

"Oh . . . up to your knees, your chest, your nose. A hundred feet over your head if we're talking about sinkholes."

"Terrific."

"Look at the bright side. The kids are in close, if this is where they were dumped. How far would you carry a body out into that pea soup?"

"What about a boat?"

Anderson chuckled morosely. "That would sure simplify things, wouldn't it, now? All we got to do to ask around if anybody saw a car with a boat lashed to the roof that night."

"I was just trying to cover all the possibilities, Mr. Anderson." Ward's eyes had hardened.

"I know, Boss," Anderson said without rancor. "I'm just beat."

"Me too."

The tops of the tallest cypresses were now yellowish-green with sunlight.

"Mr. Byrd!" Ward hollered, startling Anderson, who'd been mesmerized by the line of light inching down the trees.

"Mr. Ward?" True to form, Byrd came slogging over like the obedient little trooper he was, although his eyes were so red with fatigue it looked like they were infected.

"There's a phone back at the crossroads gas station. I want a hundred more men by noon today."

Anderson wore a shocked grin, and even Byrd looked incredulous. "You mean *Bureau* people, sir?"

"I don't care where they come from. I just need them by noon to start searching this entire swamp."

"Is that how I should put it to Memphis?"

"No, hold on a second." Ward was massaging the back of his neck with his hand. "See if we can use Navy personnel from the Meridian airbase. The important factor is that these people must be disciplined."

Unlike yours truly, Anderson thought to himself, resisting the urge to laugh at the absurdity of this proposal. "Listen, Boss— "

"Can it, Anderson. I'm asking you for the last time to stop calling me that."

He took a breath, counted to three. "Listen, *Mr. Ward,* if I was a betting man I'd wager that if the bodies are here at all, they're within a stone's throw of where we stand. I say we get some shut-eye, then come back here with waders and poles, and do the searching ourselves."

"But you'll admit that this is just an assumption."

"Well, sure."

Ward turned to Byrd again. "Please do as I asked, Mr. Byrd."

"Very good, sir."

Then Anderson could no longer contain himself: "First half the Bureau, now the Navy. Why don't you just have the goddamn Marines land down at Gulfport and start sweeping north?!"

Ward and Byrd walked away.

Sometimes a curious rejuvenation visited him just when he was ready to check himself into the hospital for exhaustion. Although his stomach was on fire from countless paper cups of coffee since returning from the swamp to the theater, he felt decent enough to pace the mezzanine and review the progress of the last six hours.

Of course, upon their immediate arrival back in town, the situation had looked hopelessly grim; reportedly three, possibly four Negro churches in the county had been burned during the night. Believing that the energies of the more diligent agents were better invested in identification work on the Ford station wagon, Ward had sent out Anderson to follow up on the sheriff's office inquiries into the burnings. He had come back an hour ago, his voice raw with weariness, and confirmed that three churches had been razed, although one of them had burned too slowly to suit the arsonists' impatience and so it had been finished off with explosives, dynamite most likely. The confusion over whether three or four churches were involved had arisen from the fact that a small outbuilding near one of the houses of worship, which was occasionally used by NAACP workers passing through, had also been fired. A caretaker at the first church to be torched had been cold-cocked. "He's conscious now," Anderson, had said, wrapping up his report, "but won't talk. Finis." Then the agent had retired to one of the theater seats and effortlessly fallen asleep.

For a moment Ward had envied Anderson, slumping there with his head thrown back and his lower jaw slack, but then he'd reminded himself that much remained to be done before the arrival of the Navy. The inspector had requested additional information and clarifications so that Director Hoover could make a statement at sixteen hundred hours to the national media concerning the discovery of the station wagon "with clear and apparent signs of foul play attending the condition of the vehicle." Ward had invented this phrase earlier, but was beginning to think it a bit overblown.

He sorely wished that he could be doing work this delicate on eight hours of sleep. He hadn't jogged since that stopover in northern Mississippi, and it was beginning to tell in a low-grade anxiousness he couldn't quite shake; he had asked the inspector for five additional agents, and then wondered upon hanging up the phone if this restive feeling had been the actual reason for the request. Composing himself, he had then phoned back the inspector with the needed information, although he had not rescinded the request for more Bureau manpower.

Now, as he paced the mezzanine, a rumble coming up through the floor stopped him in his tracks.

"Good—on time," he muttered, starting down that carpeted stairs. Byrd met him at their foot, holding out a small object.

"What's that?"

"Snakebite kit you asked me to pick up for you, sir."

"Oh yeah, thanks."

"You want me to go with you, Mr. Ward?"

"No, I'm relying on you to hold down the fort here in case Washington needs anything else. I hope to be finished out there well before dusk."

"Very good, sir."

Ward wanted to tell Byrd that he was doing a good job, but for some reason couldn't come up with the words. Instead he patted his arm on his way outside.

He boarded the first gray bus in line and introduced himself to the pimply Navy lieutenant who looked ten years younger than any of the naval reservists under his command. "Thanks for helping us out," Ward said.

"We brought the inflatable rafts," the young officer needlessly explained, for Ward had to step over one of the bundles to find the nearest empty seat. The sailors in faded dungarees were staring expectantly at him.

"We're going to look for some bodies in a swamp, gentlemen," Ward said so all could hear. The others in the following four buses could be briefed by their ensign at the site. "Driver, head south along the state highway. I'll tell you where to turn."

"Aye, aye, sir."

Ward fully realized that the men grumbling to one another. But he pretended not to notice. Besides, he understood their reluctance: who really wanted to discover three corpses after they'd been submerged for a week?

He comes home in the early evening, with the goldenness just gone out of the west. The front door is slightly ajar, which for some reason fails to register on his good mood. He scoops up the Kansas City paper on the way up the cement path, locks the door behind him, and hangs his hat and overcoat in the hall closet, which reeks of moth crystals. "Jesus, how she hates moths," He says to himself with a quizzical grin.

"Roop, is that you?" she calls from what he believes to be the master bedroom.

Yet when he opens the door, their bedroom is empty, the jalousie slats rattling in the evening breeze.

"Roop, is that you, honey?" she now calls from what he believes to be the kitchen.

But the kitchen is vacant, too, although the cold-water tap is running—something from which he draws inordinate hope.

Her final question seems to come from the tiny backyard, where she nurses her scrawny tomato plants until the first frost mummifies them: "Rupert, is that you now?"

Desperate now to reply, he rushes out the back door—and into a painful conflagration of molten light.

Anderson opened his eyes into a flashlight beam: "Turn that fucking thing off."

"Sorry," John Byrd's voice came out of the light, "Mr. Ward asked me to wake you."

A little spittle had leaked from the corner of Anderson's mouth. He dabbed it with his shirtsleeve. "Ever think of saying 'rise and shine, Mr. Anderson'?"

"No," Byrd said, completely deadpan.

"Consider it next time."

"Very well."

It was hard to believe that the good Lord would let somebody so completely lacking in humor slip through quality control. Byrd was like a bird without wings, a fish without fins. An agent who couldn't laugh was no kind of agent. Anderson slowly rose from the theater seat and stretched. He had a crick in the left side of his neck, another one in the small of his back.

Once again, the dream had left him feeling as blue as hell. "What time is it?"

"Nineteen hundred hours, Mr. Anderson."

"Seven o'clock will do just fine, John. I'm smart enough to reckon I haven't slept around the clock." He scratched his belly, wondering if the stirrings he felt there were hunger or just gas. "Just barely smart enough. Where's the boss?"

"Behind you," Ward himself said. He was sitting several rows back, reading under a student lamp somebody had clamped to the back of his seat for him.

Anderson could already tell by the man's expression that nothing had been found in the swamp, but couldn't resist asking "Zip?"

"Zip," Ward said, still reading. "Although our people working over the station wagon found a wristwatch. Presumably one of the victim's, badly burned. The hands stopped at twelve forty-five."

The phone rang, and Byrd trotted up the aisle to answer it.

Anderson noticed that Ward's clothes were a wrinkled mess. His white shirt looked like it had been washed in strong lemonade, which could only mean that he had splashed out into the ooze to show the Navy kids how to properly splash around in a Mississippi cypress swamp.

God, he was feeling foul, Anderson admitted to himself, trying to put a good face on his mood.

Byrd returned, looking worried. "Mr. Ward, may I have a word?"

"Shoot."

"That was the manager of the motel where we're staying . . ."

"Yeah?"

"Well, he wants us out. Says we're bad for business."

Ward chuckled as if he'd been expecting this all along, but then said curtly, "Buy it."

"Sorry, sir?"

"Buy the damned motel."

"How—how high can I go?"

"As high as it takes."

Wordlessly, Byrd scampered up the aisle again, and Ward went back to reading. Yet the young agent couldn't help but gloating over the blank check he had apparently just been written by the Washington brass: "That's right, Mr. Anderson," he said with a hint of a smile, "we're down here for keeps. And it's now for public dissemination—a field office is being set up in Jackson. What do you say to that?"

Anderson wasn't about to give him the satisfaction of a reply. "You have something for me to do, Mr. Ward?"

"Yes. Newsmen have been pouring into town ever since Director Hoover's statement this afternoon. Sheriff Stuckey has been shoehorned into a press conference on the courthouse steps in fifteen minutes. I'd like you to take it in."

Raymond Stuckey was staring in disbelief across his town square. His eyes could not have bulged any more had Martians just alighted there from a spacecraft. Flashbulbs were popping all about, making Clinton Pell flinch as he stood stiffly at his sheriff's side.

Anderson had taken a post on the far side of the statue of the Confederate soldier, whence he could see Stuckey but was obscured by the pedestal from camera view. He was drinking an R.C. and munching away on a Moon Pie.

"All right, folks, listen up now," Stuckey said, his voice a notch higher than usual from nervousness. Perhaps he had just realized that what would play well down at the American Legion Hall on a smoky Saturday night would not get raves with the national media. He began picking his words carefully: "I don't think finding this Ford station wagon belonging to one of the missing boys changes anything one iota . . ."

"Meaning what?" one of the newsmen demanded when Stuckey's pause grew too long.

"Meaning I still maintain this whole thing is a publicity stunt dreamed up by these NAACP and CORE and SCLC fanatics."

"Does that mean you're implicating Dr. King in this alleged publicity gimmick?"

Stuckey's eyes narrowed: he was thinking, hard. "All I will say, gentlemen, is, if the shoe fits, wear it."

"Then you have evidence that Dr. King and the Negro organizations you just named are involved in this?"

The sheriff looked down uncertainly. He was used to the homegrown variety of newsman, somebody he could sit down and do business with over bourbon and branch water, somebody who spoke his language. He seemed mystified if not outright distrustful of the direction in which these northern locusts were hornswoggling him. He finally decided on: "No comment at this time."

"Meaning you'll issue a later bulletin charging Dr. King with involvement in the disappearance of these three Voter Education Project volunteers?"

"I'm just saying that the FBI is rooting under the wrong fallen log by looking for these boys down here."

"Where should they be looking, Sheriff?"

"New York, Alaska, the North Pole—hell, I don't know. That's not my headache. It's Hoover's."

"But what if they are down here, Sheriff?"

"You got proof they is, mister?" Stuckey planted his fists on his hips. "That's enough of this. Good evening."

Another bulb popped off, and Deputy Pell acted as if it had been a muzzle flash. Sweat was glistening on his upper lip, and the veins were standing out in his thick neck. Anderson stopped smiling as he studied Pell's cratered face.

Then the deputy turned with a meaningless laugh and followed Stuckey up the courthouse steps.

7

The next morning Ward informed Anderson that he wanted to personally inspect each of the destroyed churches, to assure the congregations as best he could that something was being done to bring the perpetrators to justice.

Anderson did everything but roll his eyes, but in the end he simply asked, "You want me to go with you?"

"If you don't mind—since you've already been out to them."

They drove in silence northeast out of town on a secondary county road. It followed a powerline that hissed and crackled louder than the summer insects hiding in the lush weeds beneath it.

Ward had been surprised and even a bit disappointed when Anderson failed to argue the futility of trying to interview members of the Negro churches. He had wanted to drive home a point to him: that they would keep plugging for a break even in the face of hopelessness; that they would keeping chipping away at this frightened silence until it ultimately cracked. But the middle-aged agent had acquiesced with little more than a momentary frown. Maybe he was coming around.

Or, more probably, he was just tired, like Ward himself.

Rupert Anderson was far from being a disagreeable man, Ward mused as the countryside slipped past like a moist green blur.

Undeniably, he was even-tempered, and his few flare-ups of irritation were short-lived, lightning without much thunder.

So Ward asked himself why he so resented the man. Was it the pinpoint of suspicion that, if he could get away with it, Anderson would sabotage or at least cheerfully sidetrack Ward's investigative efforts? Or was it the former Mississippian's imperturbable conceit that nothing could be changed down here, ever?

"I got an idea," Anderson murmured, drowsily almost.

"Shoot."

"Keep going about another quarter mile, then park. We might be left with more folks to interview if we hoof it through the woods instead of barreling this sweet chariot up the church drive."

"Sounds good to me."

It seemed that Anderson did this to keep him off balance: just when Ward was sure that the man was indifferent to their assignment, Anderson would suddenly recommend some stratagem that made excellent sense. And, truthfully, Ward had been glad to have him along to deal with the Choctaw informant; he himself would have been very uncomfortable dealing with the reticent Indian.

He only wished that Anderson were solidly on his side in this thing. It would do much to assuage his own sense of unease, of being at incurable odds with the locals.

"Here okay?" he asked, pointing ahead to a

crescent of reddish dirt bowing out into the road-side weeds. In the last mile the soil had gone from black to red—an approximate demarcation between the Delta country and the central piney woods of the state, Anderson had explained earlier.

"Jim-dandy place to park."

They locked their doors and found a cow path through the chest-high growth beneath the power line. The sun was hot and the air seemed to be mostly moisture, so Ward was relieved when they reached the dappled shade of a stand of wild black cherry. Anderson paused to inspect the fruit, but then whispered that cherries this unripe were good only for a bellyache.

As they proceeded through the brushy woods, cicadas skirled in alarm at their approach, but Anderson seemed unconcerned by the noise.

Beyond the trunks of the trees the yellow-green brightness of a clearing began to unfold. Ward caught a whiff of charcoal, again that somewhat wicked stench left by a destructive fire. Yet before they could step out of the woods and start up the grassy slope that culminated in the burned church, Anderson gestured for Ward to squat down out of sight, as he himself did.

Then Ward heard what had probably halted Anderson: Negro voices drifting down from the ruin.

"Someday they come a time when we don't got to say, 'Good morning, sir, Mr. Sheriff,' " a young voice said with a self-assurance Ward hadn't heard in a Negro since arriving in Mississippi. He glimpsed the top of the boy's head over a spray of ragweed. Duck-walking a few yards to the side, he was able to fully see the intense black face. He appeared to be thirteen or fourteen years old—and very angry.

"Maybe they come a time when we don't got to say, 'Mr. Stuckey.' "

A much older voice laughed unhappily in disbelief.

"Maybe then," the boy went on, his chin high and his eyes adamant, "we just say, 'Stuckey' or 'Sheriff.' "

"What you saying?" the older voice asked, still laughing, although the laugh was now mostly a tubercular-sounding cough.

"Maybe they come a day when the sheriff won't even be a white man."

Before the old man choked to death coughing, Ward rose out of hiding and began up the slope. Anderson followed at a distance, chewing on a stalk of bluegrass.

The eyes of both Negroes were fixed on the agents.

"I wonder if we could ask a few questions," Ward said, smiling.

The boy bolted, thrashing along the edge of a shallow pond behind the charred timbers. Within seconds he was gone.

But the old man stood his ground, glumly silent, his gaze in the sooty dirt.

"I'd like to talk to the caretaker who was here last night," Ward went on.

"He gone."

"You mean to town or something?"

"Gone from the county."

"Where can I contact him, then?"

The old man shook his head at the blackened ruin, then started down the unpaved road.

"Excuse me," Anderson called from the pond, "but what kind of flower's this?"

The man stopped and turned, but said nothing.

"Prettiest damn thing," Anderson persisted. "I

see it all over this county, even in town here and there."

The old man approached, but halted ten feet shy of the agent. Rising on this toes and leaning forward slightly, he examined the flower. "That a trumpet pitcher."

"Beautiful." Anderson sniffed the horn-shaped blossom. "Don't win no contests for perfume, though. Damn near no smell at all."

"No, suh." The old man came close to smiling. "It don't smell for much."

"Sorry about interrupting your chat with your grandson."

"Aaron's my son, I'm Vertis Williams."

Anderson gave him a congratulatory nod. "Well, good for you, Vertis."

"Well, it good for somebody."

They both laughed.

Ward glimpsed an opening, although he told himself to keep it low-key, as Anderson was doing: "Why'd your boy run? Seems that wherever we go folks run away."

Vertis Williams started to answer, but then closed his mouth as he caught sight of Aaron striding out of the woods.

The boy had heard Ward's question, for he said, "Reason people don't want to talk to you is because they afraid it'll get back to the law." He stood beside his father and folded his stringy arms across his chest.

"We *are* the law," Ward said.

"Not around here you ain't," Vertis Williams said. It was more a statement of fact than a challenge.

"Look, Vertis, we're down here to find out what

happened to the three voter-registration kids. Don't you care what happened to them?"

Again the old man stared at the ground.

"Weren't those kids trying to help you?"

"What you doing here?" Aaron asked defiantly.

"I just told you, son."

"No, I mean here, talking to us."

"I don't understand your question," Ward said.

"It ain't colored folks you should be talking to."

"Who should we be talking to?"

"Aaron!" Vertis Williams barked, "Let's go. Time to go home now."

But the boy ignored his father: "You should start with the sheriff's office."

"Aaron!" the old man cried with even more alarm in his voice as he began walking down the road, flagging his hand for him to follow.

"How come you're not afraid?" Ward asked the boy.

"How come you ain't?" Then he ran after his father, but still holding his head high.

"Boy's got a point," Anderson said, idly twirling a trumpet pitcher between his fingers.

"That we should be running scared?

"No, that we oughta start with the sheriff's office."

Then Anderson started ambling back down the slope toward the Dodge.

The small frame house had a screened-in veranda. But rust had eaten through most of the screens, so Anderson figured they were little good against the mosquitoes, should Deputy and Mrs. Pell want to take the evening air on their porch. The grass needed cutting, but he drew no feeling of superiority from this observation. In those distant days when he himself had had a lawn, the grass had been in chronic need of cutting.

No sign of toys around the place, no rope swing in the old persimmon tree, he realized as he followed Ward up the cracked concrete walkway to the porch screen door.

The front door was open and through it came the sounds of a baseball game on television. A tinny roar from the crowd in St. Louis as a high fly ball drove the right fielder back to the warning track, although the announcer said that he caught it.

"Hello there?" Ward called from the stoop.

She slipped quietly from the house, but then stopped mid-veranda when she recognized Anderson. With faint awkwardness she rubbed the backs of her thin white arms.

"Good evening," she finally mustered the politeness to say.

"Good evening," Ward answered. "Mrs. Pell, is it?"

"Yes."

"I'm Alan Ward, FBI."

"Hello."

"And this is Special Agent Rupert Anderson."

"I already know Mr. Anderson, thank you."

"Hi," he said softly.

Ward shot him a questioning look, then turned back to her. "We're sorry for showing up without calling, but we'd like to ask your husband just a few more questions."

She hesitated as if this request presented her with a terrible quandary, but then said shyly, "Forgive me, please come inside, gentlemen."

"Thank you," Ward said, and Anderson echoed the same.

"Clint?" She went ahead of them into the cramped and stuffy living room, although Anderson found the cooking smells agreeable. "It's the FBI gentlemen. They want to ask you some more questions."

Pell's eyes remained fixed on the black-and-white screen, moving only to track the flight of the ball from the pitcher's hand to the catcher's mitt.

"Shall I put your dinner in the oven?"

He flicked his hand for her to take his plate from the TV tray, then sighed as he lit up a Pall Mall and shook out the match. "Leave us alone."

She left for the kitchen, her expression betraying no resentment.

It saddened Anderson a little to realize that she was used to being spoken to in this manner. Whatever his failings as a husband—and there had been many—he had never spoken abruptly to his wife. Nor had he ever struck her, not even on that awful night when she'd confessed her cheating, her complete lack of tender feelings for him.

But he had the inkling that this gentle woman got knocked around from time to time.

Clinton Pell was still refusing to acknowledge the presence of the agents. His gunbelt and uniform shirt were hanging on an oaken tree in the corner, and he was sitting in his easy chair clad only in his tan trousers and a T-shirt that was gray with sweat. His toes festered badly with athlete's foot, which pleased Anderson a little. Ringworm of the feet could be a singular torture in a climate this humid.

Pell spoke at last. "What's so goddamn important you got to bother me at home?"

"If you don't mind helping us with a few clarifications," Ward said, "I just wanted to run through your movements during the daylight hours of June 21."

The deputy took a long, heavy-lidded pull on his cigarette, but the portions of his eyes that showed were bright and cunningly alert. "June what?"

Anderson turned away to hide his disapproval. Ward was going at this all wrong. The way to get Clinton Pell's attention—and grudging respect—was to stomp on those inflamed toes and tell him he had about two seconds to get his memory in high gear. Treated decently like this, Pell would waltz the young agent all over Creation without clarifying a damned thing.

"I said June 21," Ward continued patiently.

"Was that a Saturday?"

"We both know what day we're talking about, Deputy. So let's do this civilized. The sooner we get a few answers, the sooner you get back to your game—and the sooner we get out of Mississippi."

"Then by all means, get asking," Pell said with a bitter grin.

"Now, you effected a traffic stop on a 1959 Ford Country Squire station wagon at approximately fifteen hundred hours. Is that correct?"

The deputy shrugged.

"How fast had the driver been going?"

"Eighty plus."

"Which of the three subjects was driving?"

"The nigger."

Stifling a yawn, Anderson tuned out the questioning.

Ward didn't know it, but he was spinning his wheels with Pell by doing this textbook interview. Procedural onanism. The morose deputy, like every man alive, had his buttons, but this was a piss-poor way to punch them.

He surveyed the room, looking for her touches.

The pale ash paneling had been faintly yellowed by years of cigarette smoke. Just a couple of framed pictures to study, killing time until Ward wised up. A youthful, blond Jesus gazed heavenward—the painting had probably been snipped from the cover of a church program. And then a copy of those gnarled praying hands every Southern woman seemed to hang in her house as a mute protest against her situation. A wedding picture. It sent an ache through him to see how fresh and pretty she'd been on that day—a shame to capture a woman in the instant of her beauty's zenith; forever after it's held against her like indestructible evidence of what she'd lost since and would never regain.

Then his eyes narrowed as he examined Pell in the same photograph.

Standing with his bride on one side and his best man on the other, he had hooked his thumb over his cummerbund. His crew-cut buddy was executing the same gesture.

"Hello, Dixie," Anderson whispered to himself knowingly, then drifted into the kitchen.

She glanced up from the sink, obviously uneasy with his appearance. "Hi."

"Don't let me interrupt you."

"You're not."

He chuckled needlessly. "When you've heard a question a dozen times, it gets kinda boring."

"I know. I work in a beauty parlor."

"Sure then, you know what I mean."

She went back to scrubbing the congealed grease out of a skillet.

Through the window over the sink he could see a somewhat rangy tomato patch in the backyard. Most of the visible fruit were showing orangish sunburn spots. "You don't eat together?" he asked, mostly just to end the uncomfortable silence between them.

"He works funny hours." She was reaching to rinse the scouring pad when she stopped and met Anderson's eyes. "You think that's peculiar?"

"No. Oh no. I work funny hours myself."

"But when you were growing up with your family, did you all sit down and eat together?"

"Yes," he said. "Always."

"Us too ... always. It was nice." She realized that some potato peelings were clogging the drain grate, and began collecting them for disposal in a colander that already held some carrot tops and strands of gristle.

"I eat when I'm hungry. Clint eats when he can. Can I fix you something, Mr. Anderson?"

"No, thank you. Kind of you to offer to put more bother on yourself."

"It's not a bother, honest."

"No, really," he said, although he would have liked very much to watch her prepare a meal for him. Her hands, although chapped, were pretty, and he enjoyed the way they performed small tasks. It seemed that these days, he lived in a world of blustering male hands. Making points— men were always making points with their hands. "This is a nice house." What he actually meant was that it was a familiar house; maybe when you got old enough the words became one and the same. "You lived here long?"

"I was born in the front bedroom, Mr. Anderson."

"Really, now?"

"But my daddy lost the place in a poker game one night."

"Sorry to hear that."

"Oh, it was a long time ago." She turned off the tap, but her hand remained poised on the lever. "We've been paying rent ever since."

"Well, gaming's a good man's failing."

Her eyes were suddenly hard on his. "Do you really think so, Mr. Anderson?"

He glanced away. "No. I suppose not. Daddy's playing vingt-et-un at this Cajun speakeasy up in Corinth cost us supper more than a couple times."

Seemingly satisfied by his answer, she turned back to her chores. A woman with principles, he realized, unsure exactly how he felt about this.

"What'd your daddy do, Mr. Anderson?"

"Cropper. Long line of croppers." Then he saw that Pell was glaring at him from his easy chair in the living room. Ward had either run out of questions or at last gotten the message that the deputy wasn't about to help him. He had an aimless but frustrated look about him. "Well, I gotta go, Mrs. Pell. Been real nice talking to you."

"Same here, Mr. Anderson."

"Those chops still worth eating, honey?" Pell asked. "And get me a beer, will you?"

She smiled at Anderson for a moment, then the smile died and she went to the refrigerator, opened it with a languid pull on the latch.

Returning to the living room, Anderson grinned unapologetically at Pell. "Sure a lovely wife you got, Deputy." Nothing quite as fun as bedeviling a jealous man. Particularly an abusive one. "You're a lucky fella."

Pell ignored him.

"Are we done here?" Anderson asked.

Ward nodded sourly.

But Anderson dawdled a few moments more as he regarded the television. "Time to let you get back to your game, Deputy."

"Fine," Pell groused.

"You know what they say about baseball, don't you? It's the only game there is where a colored man—"

"I know. I already heard that one."

As soon as they were outside, Ward said low, "Fifty minutes of his alibi hinges on his wife. Did she spill anything?"

"What do you mean?" Anderson asked, waiting for Ward to unlock his car door for him. The light had gone while they'd been inside, and the crickets had started up raucously.

"Weren't you interviewing her?"

"Not really."

"Then what the hell were you doing in there?"

"Wondering."

Ward hurried around the back of the Dodge, then got in, and started the engine. "Wondering? About what?"

"You know," Anderson drawled over a yawn, "you can talk about your pyramids and your UFOs, but for my money the biggest mystery in the world is why a woman like her settles on a bonehead like him." He stared back at the house. "Jesus. Did you see the wedding picture on the wall?"

"No." Ward pulled away from the curbless edge of the street after checking his side mirror for traffic.

"Pell and his best man had this cute way of hooking their thumbs in their cummerbunds with three fingers pointing down."

"So?"

"It's a sign."

"What, Masonic or something?" Ward asked.

"Try something—Klan."

"Are you surprised?"

"Seldom anymore, Mr. Ward. But if you don't mind, I'd like to get know Deputy Clinton Pell a little better. I could use the rented Ford for a couple hours."

The young agent thought about it briefly. "All right."

Waiting at the end of the darkened street for Pell to leave his house and go back on duty, Anderson had a feeling he hadn't experienced in nearly twenty years. It was a blue, restless sensation of being at loss what to do next, of being disconnected and without prospects. Maybe bumming around these past days in this timeless Mississippi burg had triggered it. The last time he could remember being hit by it had been in the autumn of 1945, when the sun had moved too slowly across the burnt-leaf-smudged sky, those pointless days when he'd been a card-carrying member of the Fifty-two and Six Club, a year-long dole for separated GIs in the form of six bucks a week. There was no work to be found, so he used the government money to eat on and buy gas for the 1934 Ford Deluxe coupe—had sitting another Ford done it to him?—his daddy had stored for him in the barn for the duration. He drove for lack of anything better to do. One night to Memphis, with the stars shining down through the November-chilled blackness. Another through the fog down to Gulfport, with bleating of the foghorns drifting miles inland to haunt him. Another over to Huntsville, daring the Alabama troopers to chase him on a road glazed with the first snowfall.

He had come home to no sweetheart: she'd dear-johned him while he was what had seemed terminally seasick on an LST tied up at South-hampton, waiting for D-Day to kick off. He had hit Utah Beach in a perverse and unhealthy mood, half wishing that the relatively mild German response there had been perkier—all the fireworks seemed to be over on Omaha Beach. But within a couple of days he'd seen enough death to quash this childish feeling. Girl or no girl, he wanted to live, and some rather nasty German kids were putting that issue in doubt.

Slumped now behind the wheel of the Falcon, he chuckled to himself. How can a man be such a damned fool? Yet that strange feeling of being both back home and apart from home was upon him again, making him sadder than he could re-member. *Your heart don't get any older than thirty, and that's the hell in aging. Your heart just don't learn.*

At last Clinton Pell sauntered out of his house and got inside his cruiser.

"Two-hour supper break," Anderson muttered. "I'd fire your lard-ass if I was your sheriff, Clint boy."

Pell unexpectedly made a U-turn in front of his house, and his high beams flooded over the Fal-con. Anderson flopped across the front seat and held his breath until the cruiser had sped past, heading west.

The agent gave Pell several hundred yards, then followed without lights, keeping a sharp eye out for kids and dogs and then deer when the houses ended and the woods began. The deputy obviously had a destination in mind; he wasn't lapsing into that patient gait a cop does when on patrol.

Anderson turned the wind wing in on himself, but the whistling rush of air was anything but cool.

Five miles out of town, according to the Falcon's odometer, Pell's brake lamps suddenly lit up and his cruiser veered off the road.

As Anderson coasted to a stop, careful not to touch his own brake pedal, he could discern a flat-roofed building set back in the pines. It was dimly illuminated and could not be identified by any signs, but a dozen cars were clustered around its front.

"I think we got us a sheriff-protected speakeasy here," he said to himself, parking on the shoulder and killing the Ford's engine.

Pell's cruiser was half concealed behind the place, the driver's door left open.

Among the tons of matériel Ward had requisitioned he'd managed to procure something useful: a pair of wide-angle binoculars, which would do a decent job of gathering the scant light spilling out the rear door of the speakeasy. Anderson removed them from their case, rolled down the passenger window, and trained the lenses on the cruiser. He prayed that Pell hadn't gone inside for a long beer.

But the deputy emerged a few minutes later. He had a half dozen good old boys in tow. They huddled around him as if he were a quarterback, their expressions intent as they listened to him. Anderson had no hope of hearing what was being said, but whatever it was, Pell had not felt comfortable relating it inside the bar.

When the deputy eventually lumbered back inside his car and hit the ignition, Anderson started up the Falcon. He turned back toward town and put the speakeasy two miles to his rear before flicking on his headlamps.

Pell's lights never shone in his mirrors: the deputy must have continued west on the road.

Anderson stopped once before town—on the banks of a roadside slough where he'd noticed some trumpet pitchers growing.

Mrs. Pell looked a little disconcerted to see him standing on her stoop—he believed. Big, dusty moths were pinging off the light fixture behind her, proving that the rust-eaten screens did no good as he'd expected. He enjoyed a well-screened porch on a hot night like this.

"My husband's not here," she said.

"Well, actually, it's you I need to talk to, Mrs. Pell." He sounded such a damn fool to his own ears, but he went on smiling as if he had all the confidence in the world, as if he'd been born with a bouquet of trumpet pitchers sprouting out of his left hand.

"Me?" She touched her upper breast just above the first button of the peach-colored housecoat she'd settled down for evening in.

"It won't take a minute."

"Well . . . I suppose, Mr. Anderson. Won't you come in, then?"

"Thank you."

She had good legs, and he wanted to look down at them, but was afraid she might suddenly wheel around and catch him appraising her. The television was going. She turned it off and gestured for him to take the sofa. It was a graceful gesture that made him feel a bit more welcome.

On the TV tray she had set an oscillating fan and before it a pan of ice cubes and water in the frail hope of cooling the wind.

"Kinda disappointing, isn't it?"

"Mr. Anderson?"

"How when the sun finally goes down it don't get that much cooler."

"Yes, disappointing." She dabbed her nape with a handkerchief she then tucked back between the seat cushion and the arm of the easy chair. "I always do so look forward to fall."

"Me too."

Her eyes turned distant. "What is it you wanted to ask me about?"

"Well, just some time things we're not too clear about." He shifted the flowers to his right hand.

"Would it be better if I put your flowers in some water while you're here?"

"Actually, they're for you." At first he was afraid that she wouldn't smile, that she'd going on looking confused and suspicious forever. But then a lovely softness came into her eyes and she accepted them.

"Why, thank you, Mr. Anderson. They're beautiful."

"Yeah, they're pretty. Don't smell like much, but they're pretty."

"Can I get you anything? Some tea?"

"That'd be great, thanks." As soon as she was gone to the kitchen to put on the kettle, he exhaled. Just sitting on Clinton Pell's worn sofa made him feel awkward, so he rose and went to the wedding photo on the wall once again.

"Oh, don't look at that. It's a terrible photograph," she said behind him.

"I wouldn't say that. Is it recent?"

"Shame on you, Mr. Anderson." She laughed, and he turned to see what her face looked like in that instant. Laughter did good things to her features; even with pretty women that always wasn't so.

"Shame for what?"

"For kidding so. We were married fourteen years ago this Christmas."

"Is this your husband's best man?"

"Yes."

"He looks familiar."

"Frank Bailey. He still lives around here. Maybe you saw him in town."

"That must be it—"

The teakettle had started shrieking, and Anderson followed her into the kitchen rather than be left with nothing to do in the living room. She turned off the gas and reached up to unlatch the dish cabinet. This time he examined her legs: excellent ones, not too slender, but not chunky in the least either. Except for the teacups, most of her dishes were Depression glass, probably inherited from her mother, but he also got the feeling that she didn't throw away much.

"How about you, Mr. Anderson? Are you married?"

"Was." He gave her a self-conscious grin as she handed him a cup. "It didn't last near as long as fourteen years. I was never home that much. I supposed she just got fed up with phone calls from Miami and postcards from Des Moines . . ." He came close to mentioning that in his absence, there had always been another man around; he'd never discussed this with anybody, and even now something made him skirt it in a favor of a dodge that heaped far less blame on his ex-wife. "I came home one evening and she was gone. I went all through the house looking for her."

Mrs. Pell looked aghast. "Did you ever hear from her again?"

"Oh, sure, through her attorney months later." He took a sip of tea, found it too hot. "I'd thought things were on the mend. But I guess they weren't." All at once, he didn't feel like talking about marriages. "Listen, my boss is concerned—"

"He seems awful young, doesn't he?"

Anderson smiled. "He sure does. He's concerned about an hour—well, fifty minutes to be exact—that your husband says he was with you."

Her eyes grew flat and cold. He was sure it was from disappointment.

"I guess he was with you, right?" Anderson finally had to ask, in what he realized at once to be the worst possible way to ask a question of this sort.

"I guess he was, Mr. Anderson."

"That's a pity. Because that means I don't have any more excuses to hang around here. And I do enjoy chatting with you, Mrs. Pell." He stood, feeling remote from her now, irredeemably screened from the glimmers of friendship she'd shown him. He had revealed himself to be a cop at heart. "Thank you for the tea."

"Thank you for the flowers," she said listlessly.

"You're welcome." He moved toward the door, listening to the padding of her bare feet on the linoleum behind him.

"Do you know what kind they are?"

"Old colored man told me they were trumpet pitchers."

"Oh sure," she said, "my daddy used to call them 'ladies from hell.' They're carnivorous." She tripped slightly on the unaccustomed word and Anderson smiled, but his smile vanished as she went on with a hard edge to her voice: "They attract so they can eat. That's not so nice, is it, Mr. Anderson?"

"I probably shoulda picked something more appropriate."

"Maybe," she said, closing the front door as soon as he had passed through it, denying herself any fresh air just to be rid of him.

He let himself out the screen door.

8

It was a combined service, four congregations jammed together because of the three churches being burned by the ofays. And when it was done and the organ had rumbled to stillness, a handful of the grown men volunteered to stay the night inside the church, because if this place went there'd be no church left for colored folks in the county.

But their women weren't happy about it and gave them worried looks and worried words that got the men grinning at one another in a funny kind of way.

One of them said that everything would be all right, that most of them had been soldiers in the war against the Nazis and would know what to do if the night riders came to fire the place. He added that night riders couldn't be much worse than Nazis, who hadn't needed liquor to get in a mood to put a hurt on you.

Aaron Williams supposed this meant that Germans had a sober meanness in them, and that was always the worst kind.

"If they come, we get on them like gravy over rice," one of the grown men said, saltylike, and Aaron liked these words very much. He would remember them, repeat them himself if he ever got the chance.

But this kind of talk got all four preachers scared up to the eyeballs, and they started hollering at the same time in those soaring voices of theirs about how they wanted no guns and no killing and—it almost sounded like—no fighting at all against the ofays if they came in the night with their Seven-Up bottles filled with gasoline and fuel oil.

Aaron didn't think much of the preachers when they said these things, and he wanted to say so, to go on record for himself. But he'd already been told by his father, Vertis, to hush—that was when he'd offered to remain with the grown men who would guard the church. He believed the same as the men who'd been soldiers against the Nazis: that guns were the right way to go if the night riders showed up to burn the church.

It was only reasonable to stop them any way they could.

But nothing was reasonable about how most of the folks, especially the preachers, felt about things. Maybe they just didn't feel anything except fear.

Half of the folks in the state were colored, but only one in twenty of them was registered to vote, because of the poll tax and the hard test the government made a Negro take to prove he was a Negro and not just a nigger.

Was this reasonable?

Yet time and again, his father and other men his age shied away from standing up to the ofays and saying that these things were no good. Why, like this evening, they'd sing "Ain't Nobody Gonna Turn Me Around" with all their heart and soul and then skedaddle in the face of the first white man to say boo to them.

Lynchings.

They were always bringing up the lynchings they had seen and those their daddies and even their granddaddies had seen—colored men hanging bloody at the crossroads with their manhood cut off, hanging their for days because their kin were too scared to claim their bodies.

And they then talked about the bright spots like those crumbs of hope were the whole pie: such as how some colored folks didn't have to pay no poll tax at all on account of how they had ancestors who'd voted in 1866 or earlier. The Grandfather Clause it was called, and some men pointed to it like it made up for all the other unreasonableness. As far as Aaron was concerned, the clause was a skinflinty little thing to offer colored folks.

"Let's go, Aaron," his father said like he wanted no back talk, and they started in the company of their neighbors down the dirt road toward the highway. But quite a ways before the asphalt, most of them—including Vertis and Aaron—turned onto a dusty footpath that zigzagged down through the woods to the lane on which most of them lived.

Aaron's mother had not come to church tonight. She never left the house when there was a promise of trouble. The past was too heavy on her mind, some folks said.

There was just enough starlight for them to pick their way, although it was so dim the usually red dust was a butterscotch color, and an old man kept thumping the ground with his walking stick to scare off any snakes that might be lurking on the path.

They had not gone far down into the woods when the same man suddenly asked, "You hear something?"

Everybody stopped mid-step, the dust floating

around their knees like ground fog, and listened to the night.

It was hard to hear anything over the crickets and the bull croakers and the bats whipping their wings against the darkness.

"I hear nothing," Vertis said.

And a woman said she didn't hear anything, either.

So the file of folks moved on again, a couple of them humming "This Little Light of Mine" to keep their nerve up.

Everybody was jittery on account of how things had been these past weeks. Aaron figured he felt no more jittery than usual and was even a little pleased by what was happening. It was all boiling to a head and things would be better afterward. Things had to get worse before they could get better.

At last they reached the lane, and the folks began straggling out like they were already thinking of their individual homes, their separate lives.

Suddenly Aaron bumped into his father's back.

The old man had halted dead in his tracks and was peering forward while waving his hands to the side for everybody else to stop, too. Aaron could make no sense of this behavior until he began picking out some shapes in the night that seemed nothing like trees or bushes or other familiar things along the unlit lane.

"Who's there?" Vertis called.

But nobody answered.

Aaron realized that the shapes were cars and pickup trucks, a whole long line of them parked along the shoulder of the lane. Leaning against these vehicles were men who gave the air that they'd been patiently waiting for some time.

The men were wearing white hoods—not the pointy kind worn with white robes Aaron had seen once while spying on a big Klan gathering from the pines, but flour sacks with black holes cut in them for a man's eyes and mouth.

"Run!" Vertis cried, although he himself could not do so because of his rheumatism and bad lungs.

The men gave out a frightening Rebel yell as they charged after the folks.

Aaron stood his ground beside father.

"Get, son!"

He could feel the pounding of the white men's feet through the ground. It came up through his ankles and knees, and made them feel weak. But he didn't run, not even when Vertis shoved him toward the side of the lane.

Then one of the hooded men was standing before them, with either a pickax handle or a baseball bat in his hands.

"Don't hurt my boy," Vertis said. "Please don't hurt my boy."

"Y'all been told before, nigger," the voice growled like it belonged to a beast instead of a man. But Aaron knew whose voice it was. "Y'all been told."

"Told what, suh?"

"To go opening your boot-lips to any federal men."

"I said noth—"

Then Vertis was struck alongside his head. He went down fast and made no sound.

Aaron wasn't sure which was more terrible: to see his father unconscious in the middle of the lane, or to realize that somebody had talked about their chance meeting with the FBI men. Only colored folks had known about that.

He started to cringe, waiting for the blow and the darkness that would surely follow. But then something made him kneel as if in church: "I know you, Lester Cowens."

Instead of the stick, Aaron felt a boot slamming against his ribs. It took the wind out of him, but still he was glad he'd said what he had.

He had told Cowens that his hood did no good. The days of pretending that it did were gone forever.

After the naval reservists had come up empty-handed in the Choctaw swamp, Ward felt that he personally was the target of the contemptuous glee in town. The good sheriff had insisted that the three voter-registration volunteers would not be found in these parts, and now the green G-man was only confirming this assertion.

Not quite. As far as Ward was concerned, that portion of the swamp immediately around where the Ford station wagon had been found was eliminated as the body disposal site. But there were many more swamps, sloughs, and creeks to be searched, and he intended to go through every last one of them until the bodies were found.

Somehow, that the Country Squire had been ditched in water suggested to him that the volunteers had been concealed in the same way. So he called upon the U.S. Navy once again, since water was their specialty, and commenced a search operation by weekend sailors under his command of every creek and slough crossed by the state highway between town and the turnoff onto the Choctaw reservation. His premise was that the suspect or, more probably, the suspects, had dumped the corpses as conveniently and quickly as possible before considering what to do with the Ford wagon.

Naturally, because the search was being conducted near the main north-south artery in the county, it attracted onlookers from its first hour. By mid-morning they had become numerous and boisterous enough to require crowd control. And the media was not helping by encouraging comments from the more vociferous bystanders—nothing like some cracker spewing American fascism to liven up the six o'clock news.

Ward had long since tired of letting Jackson play cat-and-mouse with him: the governor's office would contend that a mess of catcalling yahoos sounded like a county concern, and then the sheriff would say that anything involving a state highway had to be handled by Mississippi troopers, adding that his limited manpower pool was already being strained to the limit by these federal shenanigans.

No, Ward had finally learned how to circumvent these antics: he had Washington telephone the governor and politely say, "Our people down your way need some state troopers for crowd control." And when the governor mumbled something about that being the county sheriff's business and how reluctant he was to intervene in local affairs, Washington had been instructed to utter just two words: "Little Rock." In the fall of 1956, in the face of outright defiance by the governor of Arkansas over ending school segregation, President Eisenhower had ordered one thousand paratroopers of the 101st Airborne Division to Little Rock and simultaneously put the Arkansas National Guard under federal command, so the governor could not continue to use his state's militia as an instrument against integration. It had not looked good for Arkansas: the photos of combat-outfitted paratroopers, the same patriots who'd jumped into Normandy just a dozen years before, with fixed bayonets making sure little Negro girls with pigtails got to class unmolested by the rednecks howling at them.

"Little Rock" had apparently done the trick, for about an hour after Ward had telephoned Washington from the gas station where they'd met with the Indian informant, five Mississippi state troopers convoyed to the search site. Their sergeant reported to Ward without smiling or offering to shake hands, but he did announce to the crowd in the booming voice of a drill instructor that "fooling" with the FBI and the Navy was now ended. Then he and his men adjourned to the shadow of a wild magnolia tree, where they glumly chewed and spat tobacco onto the big leathery leaves that had fallen onto the shoulder of the road.

Their presence did not completely end the derision, but it did tone it down to the usual racist humor Ward had constantly heard since landing in Memphis over a week ago:

"Y'all wanna find that nigger, hah?" a peckerwood crooned at the sailors, who were waist deep in the slime of a scarcely flowing stream. "You just throw a welfare check atop that water there—why he'll reach up and grab it."

The trooper sergeant smiled for an instant, but then spat and said, "That's enough there, you hear?"

"Yes, sir," the peckerwood said with mock solemnity, then realized with unease in his face that he was being filmed by the CBS crew. His confidence was quickly restored: "Folks round here get pretty riled once you get 'em going. They'll take up the gun again—just like they done before. Like the ol' song says, 'Three hundred thousand Yankees is stiff in Southern dust.' Push us too damn hard and it'll happen again. I ain't looking forward to it, but I'm just being honest about what I know to be the God's truth about people down here."

"This is all an insult," another man chimed in, who by virtue of a similar overbite and weak chin was probably the first peckerwood's kinsman. "If these boys had gone missing up in New York, you think the FBI and the United States Navy'd be rummaging round for them like this? Hell no!"

"Hell no!" other voices echoed, loud enough for the troopers to stand straight and make sure their campaign hats were on square.

Yet at that moment Ward could hear another local, a farmer with hair burned a pale gold by the summer sun, being interviewed by the NBC crew. Standing sheepishly with his hands buried in his coverall pockets, he was calmly saying, "They say we must eat together, use the same restrooms as the nigras. Well, that's a hard proposition for some Mississippi folks. For me too, I suppose. But we saw it coming. The nigras here been treated awful bad for a long time, don't you know."

When the camera had moved on, Ward stared at the man until he became aware of it and returned his gaze. He wanted to shake the farmer's hand, for in him was the kernel of hope that this one day might change, that Mississippi was not the lowest level of hell after all.

But Ward didn't approach him.

He now fully understood how his approval could get a decent man hurt, murdered even.

*   *   *

"A couple hotheads with a bellyful of moon-shine rough up a few folks in a scuffle," Mayor Lyle Tilman said to the reporters who'd backed him up onto the steps of the Masonic Hall, "and all of a sudden it's national news!"

"These people were more than roughed up, Mayor," the ABC man interjected before Tilman could really get rolling. "One of the women has a broken arm, an old man a concussion. What is the sheriff's office doing about this clear case of assault and battery?"

"They're doing plenty, gentlemen. Now let's particularize here. There are eight hundred serious crimes a day on the streets of New York City. Eight hundred." Tilman paused to grin at the enormity of it. "And did you know that down here in Mississippi we have the lowest crime rate in America?" He gestured with his stubby little cigar at the reporter closest to him. "May I ask where you're from, suh?"

"*Time* magazine."

"No, I mean where were you born and raised?"

"Minnesota."

"Lovely country, lovely indeed. Some years ago, I spent a month one night in Minneapolis." This earned the mayor a few grudging chuckles from the press, even Anderson found himself smiling for the first time that day. "But all funning aside, suh, in all honesty how'd you have felt if bus loads of Ivy League types and Chicago nigras with radical socialist ideas had suddenly poured into your lovely state?"

"As I recall, Mayor, we didn't make it a practice of beating Negroes as they walked home from church."

"And are you suggesting that we do?"

"It happened last night," the *Time* man said.

"Yes, it did. But you tell me now—if the entire Secret Service and Dallas police department couldn't protect the president of these United States, how in hell are we supposed to protect a few nigras?" Tilman's piggish eyes had begun to show his rising anger. "And did all of Texas kill Kennedy? You know as well as I do that one nut did the deed on his lonesome. And I'm telling you again, last night wasn't nothing but some white trash drinking too much moonshine—"

"Mr. Townley . . ." a reporter interrupted, having both recognized the grand wizard standing behind the mayor and concluded that Tilman was only going to repeat himself from now on. "To what do you attribute these attacks on Negro church people?"

Clayton Townley chuckled as he dropped his cigarette underfoot and stubbed it out with the toe of his gator-skin boot. "I think you're talking to the wrong fella, suh. I can't rightly speak for these good folks. I'm from Tupelo, just down here on business and hoping to rub elbows with my lodge brothers—if you'll be so kind as to let go of them."

"Would that be Klan business, Mr. Townley?"

The affable expression ran off his face. "Suh?"

"Aren't you a spokesman for the White Knights of the Ku Klux Klan?"

Anderson shifted forward so he wouldn't miss the precise look in Clayton's eye when he lied through his teeth: he might have occasion to play poker against him someday.

"I told you, young fella. I am a businessman from Tupelo. I'm also a Mississippian. And an American with honorable war service in the United

States Army. And I'm sick to the eyeballs of us Mississippians having our views distorted by you people. I am sick—!"

"Did you recently sign a petition demanding that the U.S. withdraw its recognition of the state of Israel?" a reporter butted in, having sniffed out Townley's careless anger at a distance of thirty feet.

"We do not support the Jews because after all these centuries they continue to reject our Savior and because they control the banking cartel that is at the root of what we call communism today."

"What about the Catholics?" the newsmen were eating it up: it wasn't often they got this close to the jaws of such a ravening bigotry. "Why are you opposed to them?"

"We do not believe we can trust the papists as bona fide Americans because their first loyalty is to a Roman dictator. As far as Turks, Mongols, Tartars, Orientals of all slants"—he smiled through his rage at his own little joke, then went on even more venomously when nobody laughed—"and Negroes—because they are not progressive peoples and it is foolish and irresponsible of us to think that they can take an active part in our Anglo-Saxon democracy. In fact, it would be cruel of us to expect so much of them!" Alerted by a tug on his elbow, Townley leaned over so the mayor could whisper in his ear. He nodded, then smiled at the newsmen as if to say that no harm had been intended. "I guess you got me going, boys, but now it's time to wet my whistle. Y'all have a pleasant afternoon, now. And don't get too much sun on that nice white skin. It'll kill you sure as cholera." Then he ducked inside the hall.

Anderson lingered a few minutes longer among

the reporters, mostly just to savor their disbelief. Then he continued his early afternoon stroll down the sidewalk.

Curiously, Ward had saddled him with nothing to do today, which meant one of two things: either the young agent was too busy with his own leads to think of anybody else, or he actually trusted Anderson to develop his own information. He wanted to believe the latter reason if only because he desired a smoothly working relationship with whomever he was assigned, but the former reason was probably closer to the truth.

Last night Ward had decided to bunk with Byrd at the motel, explaining only that he intended to work late from now on and didn't want to disturb Anderson's beauty sleep. He tried not to make too much of Ward's relocating, but it rankled. An agent didn't switch roomies unless there was a problem—everybody knew this from experience.

He was nearly to the edge of town when he noticed Pell's cruiser parked in front of a Quonset hut, probably bought surplus from the Army Air Corps after it deactivated its wartime base between here and Hattiesburg. A sign over the door read:

CITIZENS' COUNCIL SOCIAL CLUB
MEMBERS ONLY

"What the hell," he muttered, coming to the conclusion that he could think of nothing better to do at the moment than lean on Clinton Pell. The only thing was, he wasn't quite sure why he felt this way.

The front door had been propped open with a brass flagstaff stand, and the sounds of jovial conversation were flowing out on clouds of tobacco smoke. But as soon as he stepped inside, the round-roofed place went quiet.

"I shoulda been a schoolteacher," Anderson said to the ten or so men sitting inside at little cocktail tables. "You open?"

"You gotta be a member to drink here," Pell said, chewing on a thumbnail.

"I had me a handwrote invitation. Musta lost it someplace."

Pell's indifferent gaze swept over to the bartender. "Give him a beer, Frank." He took his boot off the chair opposite him.

Anderson sat down and nodded his thanks to the bartender for setting the small mug before him. "God, it's good to be in a dry country once again."

"Why's that, Hoover boy?" Pell asked.

"Well, drinking and gambling should be done on the sly. Otherwise they tend to lose their luster. Take your preachers down here—do they really wanna give sin a black eye? If they do, they're going about it all wrong." Anderson took a careful sip, his eyes strangely humorless as they fastened on Pell's acne-pocked face. "Ranting and raving against sin only makes it sound all the more interesting. If they want to make some real headway against it, the preachers oughta advertise sin to be as common and boring as Sunday school. Give everybody all he can use. Hell, in no time you'd have a whole town full of nothing but saints."

A clink echoed across the silent Quonset hut as somebody dropped a dime into the jukebox. Hank Williams was resurrected from the dead, if only for as long as ten cents would last. For once, Anderson felt untouched by Hank's music.

"When I was sheriff," he went on, doggedly now, "almost half my take-home was from levying informal taxes on illegal jukes like this old Wurlitzer. I'd think jukes still haul in a pretty penny, that and winking at bootleggers."

"I wouldn't know," Pell said sullenly.

The bartender turned an empty chair around and eased into it, his flinty eyes never leaving Anderson's face as he slid down.

"Frank Bailey," Pell introduced him.

"Pleasure," Anderson said, "I'm Roop—"

"I know who you are."

Anderson nodded at his nearly empty glass. "You got anything stronger than beer, Frank?"

"No."

"You sure, now?"

"Yes."

"A pity. In my county there was a joy-juice still in every hollow, every damn basement too. It's really a simple matter of making it. All you need is a little corn and some sugar and a pot to boil it in." Anderson chuckled as if in remembrance, his upward gaze watching a horsefly dodging the blades of the ceiling fan. "You know, once I tried to roll the fingerprints of a fella who'd had his hands stuck in a mash barrel all his life. Skin was burnt clean off. It was like trying to get friction ridges off an egg—"

"We ain't interested in your Hill country stories, Anderson." Pell took the bait at last. "You never was Delta folk, but ain't even Hill folk anymore. Christ, you ain't even a Mississippian. Right, Frank?"

"Right."

It didn't show in his face, but the agent was gratified. He had been fumbling for buttons. Clinton Pell's buttons. "What kind of stories are you interested in, then, Deputy?"

Pell blew out a long stream of smoke, then smirked at him through the pall. "Is this all just a paycheck to you?"

"And if it is?"

"Well, I still wouldn't respect you worth a shit. But I'd understand, maybe."

"Why'd you up and leave Mississippi anyways?" Frank Bailey demanded, as if Anderson had defected to the Soviet Union instead of just moving out of the state.

"I'd accomplished what I'd set out to do."

"And what was that?" Pell asked contemptuously.

"Fired all the deputies who took two-hour supper breaks or boozed it on duty or shook down drunks for cash."

Pell leaned forward and with a loud thunk planted his elbows on the tabletop. "If that's how you feel, I'd be obliged if you'd finish that last swallow in your mug and get outta here."

"Yeah," Frank Bailey said, "get on back to your commie nigger-loving bosses up North."

"I take it you don't know much about Mr. Hoover. This is the first time I've ever heard him called a commie."

"Well, it won't be the last." Frank Bailey grasped the back of his chair and stretched with a satisfied groan, as if he were giving a good account of himself in the discussion. "We got us five thousand hi-de-hoe niggers in this county what ain't registered to vote yet. And they ain't never gonna get registered—unless it's over my dead body or a mess of dead niggers."

"You'd kill, Frank?" Anderson asked. "Is that what you're telling me?"

"Damn straight. And I wouldn't give it no more thought than wringing a cat's neck."

"What about the law?"

"Shit, there ain't a court in Mississippi who'd ever convict me. You know that, Anderson."

The agent turned to Pell. "What about you, Deputy? What do you say to wringing a couple necks?"

"Keep pestering my wife, Hoover boy, and yours is gonna be the first."

Anderson's body tensed, and that was enough to make Frank Bailey seize his forearm and pin it to the table. The agent stared down at the man's grasp as if disbelieving that anyone would do such a thing to him.

"Get this straight, corn hole," the bartender hissed. "You tell your queer-ass boss he ain't never gonna find those civil righters down here. So you might as well pack your bags and get on North—!"

Anderson slammed his beer mug against the side of Bailey's head. The thick glass didn't shatter, so the flow of blood was little more than a trickle that wound around his ear and down his neck. When the man's eyes fluttered back for an instant, Anderson thought he was going down for the count. But he stayed in his chair, although with a dazed expression.

"Now *you* get this straight, shit-kicker," Anderson said quietly but angrily. "You have obviously confused me with somebody else, because I make it a habit of leaving anywheres when I'm damned well ready."

Suddenly Pell kicked away from the table, overturning it with a crash, and gave himself room in which to draw. Yet he hesitated with his hand on the backstrap of his revolver and finally decided to leave his wheelgun holstered.

"That gun just for show, Deputy?" Anderson asked, rising from his chair. "Or do you get to shoot people every once in a while?"

Pell said nothing, his jaws locked.

"Afternoon, gentlemen." Anderson walked out, taking his time about it.

9

Ward waited a full two hours after deciding what he would do with Anderson before summoning him.

He did this because he wanted his outrage to be under tight wraps. An experienced supervisor did not undertake a disciplinary matter until he had given himself ample time to cool off and collect his thoughts. Otherwise, what should be a constructive encounter would quickly deteriorate into a shouting match between peers—the very thing Anderson would try to bring about.

Over the past several days, with the case no closer to solution, Ward had felt his temper building. It was not the good anger that had made him suddenly quit his college fraternity when it refused to allow a Negro premed student to rush. Instead it was the brash and willful anger his parents had tried, perhaps unsuccessfully, to chastise out of him. Twice in high school he had been suspended for fighting—the only blemishes on a flawless academic and athletic record. But in the eyes of his parents, those two lunchroom donnybrooks seemed to have effaced all of his other achievements. He regretted them more than anything else in his life, for they were undeniable proof that in his heart he was not a gentle man, that he lacked the self-control of a complete man. Perhaps that is why he had joined the Bureau: it was just one more family that prized self-control over all other virtues. The Bureau, with all of its rules and rigidity, was helping him overcome his secret flaw, and if for no other reason deserved his devotion.

He was waiting for Anderson in the house of the theater, having taken one of the aisle seats in the last row.

Several rows below him sat the six newly arrived agents, attentively viewing a film he had arranged for them as part of their orientation. Four of them had never been assigned to the south before, and they seemed somewhat bemused as they watched klansmen strut around in their flowing white robes, backlit by a flaming cross. "The Negroid man is awful backward now," a former grand wizard said, pausing to rub his eyes because some smoke had gotten into them—the agents chuckled. "The Caucasoid race is not so. Far from it. So how can we tolerate these mixers who are shoving us one and all to the brink of wholesale mongrelization? You see, suh, we are the last protectors of white womanhood. And so your obligation is a heavy one. For as goes white womanhood, goes the future of the white race."

"Is this one taken?" Anderson asked from the aisle, pointing at the seat beside Ward's.

"No," he said.

Anderson sidled past Ward's knees, clutching a small brown paper sack of nuts. Pecans they proved to be, when the agent fished one out and cracked the shell between his back molars.

With a wave Ward declined the offer to have one.

"Have I missed much?" Anderson asked. He didn't quite sound as breezy as usual, which Ward took as a good sign.

"Not much. You have breakfast yet?"

"Sure enough. A jim-dandy one. I think that waitress is sweet on me."

The two men lapsed into silence as the grand wizard continued to brief the camera on the future of race relations in America.

"What happened yesterday?" Ward finally asked quietly.

"Little of this, little of that."

Ward gritted his teeth together, silently counted to five before continuing: "It was on Jackson radio this morning, Mr. Anderson. Everybody and his cousin—the governor of this state, Mayor Tilman, and even 'respected Mississippi entrepreneur' Clayton Townley—fuming about how the FBI, on running out of credible leads, has started resorting to intimidation."

"Oh," Anderson harrumphed. "You tell me all this fuss is over some good old boy getting conked for talking sass?"

"Then you admit striking a party by the name of Franklin Bailey?"

"Shit, Frank Bailey's no party. He don't even amount to an ice cream social."

"I'm completely serious, Mr. Anderson."

The agent looked aside at him, his face a paltry gray from the reflection off the silver screen. "So am I."

"Did you strike Bailey?"

"Sure, I hit him upside the head with a beer mug. He didn't seem to mind. Matter of fact, he turned quite agreeable after I calmed him down that way."

Ward nodded: he was relieved that Anderson had told him the truth. Had he done anything but that, Ward would have initiated formal disciplinary action against him—routing the paperwork directly to the Washington level.

"Do you realize, Mr. Anderson, that your behavior could be construed as assault with a deadly weapon under a statute of the Mississippi penal code?"

"What, beer a deadly weapon?" Anderson cracked another pecan husk between his back teeth. "You might have a point there—it sure as shit killed my daddy."

These were red flags, and Ward steeled himself against responding to them. Again he inwardly counted to five, his eyes gravitating to the screen once again.

"It's my understanding they don't desire to be called colored no more," the grand wizard was rambling on, "even though one of their communist organizations, the NAACP, still's got the word smack dab in the middle of it. Some of the more sensitive type don't even want to be called Negro. So to avoid offending these folks, we have resorted to referring to them as BLUMFs." He offered the camera a wink before going on: "That's Big-Lipped Ubangi Mother Fuckers."

"Another charge has been inferred against you," Ward said.

"What's that?" That I littered on my way out the social club?"

"No, that you've been harassing Deputy Pell's wife."

For the first time Anderson seemed off balance.

He started to say something, but then suddenly rose and rushed out into the lobby.

Following him, Ward found him pacing in front of the candy counter, his ordinarily placid face as tight as a drumhead.

"Did she herself say that, Ward?"

"No."

"Who, then?"

"Pell."

"Ah," Anderson said as if that cleared everything up. "He's a lying son of a bitch."

"I'd tend to believe you more than Pell—"

"Why, thank you."

But Ward was not finished: "*If* you can report some progress with Mrs. Pell about those fifty minutes."

Ward thought for an instant that Anderson was going to come at him, swinging. Even though the agent was grinning, it was an incensed grin, completely lacking in humor, and he was tilting his head from side to side like a enraged bull.

Yet he didn't advance on Ward, and a few moments later he shook out the fist his right hand had formed. "Your problem, Ward, is that you don't know when to speak and when to shut up. And that makes you a fool to these people."

Ward decided to let him talk, even if his talk tended toward insults. He wanted to have some idea of what Anderson was feeling. Then he might be able to better use the man as the investigation became more involved—and politically explosive. He could still visualize a place for Anderson in this effort, if only he could be reached.

"Mrs. Pell isn't going to say anything her husband doesn't want her to say. Not a damn thing. So what the devil am I supposed to do about it?

Slap it out of her? Not this sweet lady. I'll lean on anybody you can name down here, Ward. But not her. Do we understand each other, Ward?"

"Then what are you accomplishing by calling on her? Killing time?"

"What's that supposed to mean?" Anderson asked, reaching into his bag of pecans once again.

"It means I believe your heart hasn't been in this assignment from day one."

Anderson shrugged as he spit a shell onto the worn, greasy carpet.

"Is that the way it is?"

"I don't know how it is, Ward."

"Which indicates to me that you have no expectation things can be changed in Mississippi."

"As usual, you got it dead wrong," Anderson said, temper coming into his voice again. "Can't you understand that 'I don't know' amounts to a conviction down here?" He jabbed his forefinger toward the house, and Ward immediately understood that he was referring to the robed figure they'd been watching on the big screen: "That old peckerwood—he knows. For chrissakes, man, he knows down to the marrow of his bones. I don't, and that makes me something of an outsider here. But you just figure I'm one of them walking bed sheets, and that's that. So go fuck that old cracker, Roop Anderson, and let's get on with the war. You lump us all together, just like some folks do the colored. There's all kinds of prejudice in this world, Ward. But you just haven't had your nose rubbed in yours yet."

"Maybe," Ward said in the same level voice, "but I try not to let my prejudices affect my performance."

"The hell you don't."

Ward just stared at him.

"Know what gets me about you?" Anderson asked. "You really want to know?"

"Please tell me."

"You don't give a rat's ass if this case gets solved. You just want to be able to say later that you ramrodded the biggest operation the Bureau ever mounted south of the Mason-Dixon line. That's what you want to take out of this, *Boss*."

At last Ward felt a hot surge of anger, and he might have answered Anderson had not John Byrd barreled through the front glass doors at the moment.

"Mr. Ward," he said breathlessly, "there's a demonstration coming up the street."

"Klan?"

"No, sir, Negroes and sympathetic whites. They have an escort of state troopers."

"State or county officials give us notice of this?" Ward asked.

"No, although a parade permit must have been issued."

Ward's gaze floated around the lobby while he considered what do do. It settled on Anderson. "I want you to monitor this parade, Mr. Anderson, and make sure there are no violations of federal law."

He nodded and started out the door.

But Ward stopped him: "Henceforth, Mr. Anderson, you are to consider yourself under my personal supervision. Any departures from professional conduct will be reported in writing to Washington. Do I make myself clear?"

The man gave him a Boy Scout salute.

*   *   *

Anderson arrived on the sidewalk in time to see a six-and-a-half-foot trooper in a blue hardhat begin snatching small American flags out of the hands of Negro high school kids, who were smartly decked out in their marching-band uniforms but bore no instruments—probably because the parade permit had disallowed such a "public nuisance" as music by Stephen Foster and John Philip Sousa.

Close by at curbside, a peckerwood in a Cardinals baseball cap and a pack of smokes rolled up in the sleeve of his T-shirt suddenly hollered at a colored baton girl in a spangled blue outfit: "Hey, bitch! Why don't you go back to Atlanta or wherever 'tis you belong!"

She had been smiling heretofore, but that stopped.

Anderson shuffled over and bumped the peckerwood into a lamppost, hard. "Oh sorry!"

"What the hell you doing, mister?!"

"Please accept my apologies. I don't know what to say. I should be more careful."

"Damn right!"

Anderson moved on, smiling. They were exhilarating, these little revenges. And they seemed to be the only antidote to the dark and confused feeling that had come over him in the past forty-eight hours. It had felt great to mash that beer mug into Frank Bailey's face. And it had proved something vital as well: that a good number of these yokels would back off if only you showed that you had bigger fangs than they did. Ward would never understand. He had been shot once and now probably figured that he had violence down pat. Hell, he didn't know a thing about it. Watch fifty men wiped out in ten minutes, men trying to fight tanks with small arms, and you got an inkling of what the game was really about. But Ward didn't have a clue. He was one of those guys who confused getting hurt with doing the hurting.

"Let it go, Roop," he said to himself, "let it go before you wind up on the carpet with the inspector handing you a jar of Vaseline."

What the peckerwood had hollered about Atlanta made sense. Most of these marchers looked to be out-of-towners bused in by the Council of Federated Organizations. The local Negroes had suffered too much lately to have much of a stomach left for a parade.

"Go home, niggers!" an old woman with milky blue eyes cried.

"Excuse me, ma'am," Anderson said politely, "please don't do that."

"Why not?"

"Your face looks like stewed prunes when you shout that way."

She turned her hunched back to him, and he ambled on a few steps only to realize that he was in front of the beauty parlor.

He halted, but then continued his stroll again— only to shuffle to a stop ten feet later.

"Ain't nobody run me off yet," he said at last, then made for the front door even though he didn't have a thing in mind to say to her.

He asked himself why he was doing this, and the best answer he could come up with was that he wanted to see for himself that she really had not complained about his supposedly harassing her. Except for a couple of awkward moments, she was not troubled by his company—he would have staked his life on it.

The place was empty except for her and Connie. She was doing her young assistant's hair.

"You lied, Constance Faye," Anderson said sternly.

"Say what, now?" Connie's face remained immobile, but her eyes shifted to regard him.

"You told me you got your hair done in Jackson."

"You're right." She giggled as best she could without moving her head. "I lied."

Mrs. Pell refused to glance up from her work. A bobby pin was tucked in the corner of her lips.

Standing there, feeling as stupid and gangly as a kid in a varsity jacket, he realized what a delicate perplexity he had stumbled into. He didn't want her to think that he'd dropped by the night before last to make a pass at her, although the God's truth was that he had liked her from the first time he'd seen her. On the other hand, he didn't want her to think that his motives had been entirely dictated by the Bureau, that he had behaved tenderly toward her because he needed to find out about the fifty minutes her husband was claiming to have spent with her on the night the three kids disappeared.

"Anybody care for a pecan?" he asked, just to stir up the unpleasant silence.

"I'm sick to death of pecans," Mrs. Pell finally spoke.

"Funny, you don't look it."

She glared at him.

"Sorry, sometimes I must sound fresh to you. I don't mean to."

"Then you should be more careful in the future, Mr. Anderson. This morning my husband arrested a colored boy for talking fresh to a white lady."

"Seems a small thing to go to jail for."

She held his gaze, strangely. "Oh, jail's the least of that boy's worries. He's going to be released tonight at ten." Then she went back abruptly to Connie's wet hair.

"Say," the girl piped up, "how come you guys ain't asked me no questions? Seems everybody in town's got grilled except me."

"We're saving you for the rack we got on special order."

She laughed. "I got my own rack already. You just send over one of them pretty FBI boys I seen coming in and out of the old theater."

"Constance Faye," Mrs. Pell warned, sounding serious, "you behave yourself."

"I was just kidding." Connie quickly changed the subject. "How come you're not out watching the parade, Mr. Anderson?"

"Oh, honey, I haven't cared much for parades, since Paris, I guess." He gazed out the open door upon ranks of middle-aged Negro clergymen flashing past. Most of them must have been in the military, for they were marching pretty well for civilians: in step and eyes forward, proudly. Colored troops had always been the sharpest marchers. "See, after liberating the city, the Army put on this big show for the Frenchies. They marched thousands of us right up the Champs-Elysées. The people were cheering their heads off, and the prettiest girls I'd ever seen outside Mississippi were blowing kisses at us right and left. Damn, but if you couldn't smell the wine and lipstick on the breeze." Still looking outside, he bit the inside of his cheek for a moment. "But the Army wouldn't let us stop. Not even for twenty minutes. We kept marching right up to the tailgates of the trucks that hauled us to the front. Five hours later we were back in the thick of it. That was the worst damn feeling, you know—to hear the sound of that happy crowd getting fainter and fainter to our backs."

He turned only to see that the faces of the two women had gone as still as portraits. Laughing in embarrassment, he said, "Look at me, lecturing about ancient history. Sorry for interrupting your morning."

With that, he left.

"How'd you hear about this?" Ward asked, sipping coffee from a Thermos bottle lid. When Anderson didn't answer right away, he turned toward him: "If you don't mind saying."

"Well," the agent drawled, "you talk to folks, you can't help but hear things."

"This isn't a certain investment paying off?" Ward smiled in what he hoped would be taken as a good-natured way, but Anderson remained somber.

"I don't have any investments down here anymore." Then he gazed through the windshield of the rented Plymouth Fury once again.

Ward had exchanged the white Ford Falcon for the Plymouth when white kids had begun jeering at it. He figured that it was time for a new surveillance car, although even this new one would have an undercover value of only a day or so. The town was too small for a strange car to blend into traffic, and besides, how was he to disguise his impeccably groomed agents?

All at once Anderson sat up and braced his hands on the dashboard.

Ward tracked his stare to a dark-colored Lincoln Continental that had just pulled up to the jail entrance of the courthouse. The brake lamps faded, and Sheriff Stuckey lumbered out, checking in all four cardinal directions.

He obviously failed to see the Plymouth Fury parked in the shadow of the hardware store across the square. A jaundiced sliver of moon was throwing just enough light to give the townscape some contrast, and Anderson had suggested how to take advantage of it, citing his infantry days. Ward had gone along with the recommendation, even going so far as to tell Anderson that he valued the man's tactical experience. He wanted him to know that there was still a slot for him in this investigation, if only he would accept it.

Stuckey pushed through the jail door and was gone from sight.

Anderson sat back again.

Ward offered him some coffee, but he declined. "No, thanks. Well, Stuckey got a phone call. I wonder who else did."

"I have a feeling that those who did would make excellent candidates for our suspects."

"Me too. But there's a big difference between us knowing and a jury of their peers convicting."

"Then how do we do that?"

"Get a conviction?"

Ward nodded as he raised the lid to his lips and blew across the surface of the steaming coffee. The night was too hot for coffee, but it was already ten o'clock and he might not be able to rest his head on a pillow until dawn.

"If we want a conviction," Anderson said, "we may have to ask the devil for a little help."

"Sell our souls so justice can be done?"

"Wouldn't be the first time, Mr. Ward."

The jail door swung open, and Ward half expected to see Sheriff Stuckey reemerge. But it was a slender Negro youth who stepped out into the night, clutching a paper shopping sack. He was closely followed by Deputy Clinton Pell, who shouted something at him that was garbled by distance, then gave him a parting shove.

"Thanks for your patronage, son," Anderson muttered.

Pell went back inside and drew down the shade on the glass upper half of the door.

The youth reacted to neither the taunt nor the manhandling. He followed the sidewalk to the corner, crossed the empty street without looking, and ventured out into the square. Under a lamppost he halted and opened the sack. From it he took his wallet, comb, and other effects, then tucked them in his trouser pockets. Finished with the sack, he carefully folded it up as if he intended saving it.

"Thrifty kid," Anderson said. "His mama trained him well."

"What do you actually think they charged him with? Disturbing the peace?"

"Hell, boys like Stuckey and Pell don't feel the need to mince words in their booking blotter. They probably put down 'colored in public.' "

The youth was at the far corner of the square when headlights flooded over him from an alley, startling him.

"Start your engine," Anderson said.

"Why—?"

"Just start the goddamned car, Ward."

As he poured his coffee out the window with one hand and turned the key with the other, Ward saw the headlights advance on the youth, who began to bolt down the sidewalk. But he had taken no more than three strides when a GMC pickup pulled alongside. A large man jumped from the cab and seized him by the arms.

"Shit," Anderson said, "one of us shoulda been tailing the kid on foot."

Ward took his eyes off the youth for only as long as it took him to negotiate the first corner of the square, but when he looked across the quad again both the Negro and the pickup had vanished.

"They took the state highway south," Anderson said. He had unholstered his revolver and was holding it against his thigh.

For a fleeting moment Ward felt the dull, intractable ache in his shoulder. He jammed the automatic shift down into low and accelerated until the next corner forced him to slow.

"Hurry, man."

"I'm going as fast as I can," he told Anderson tersely.

Yet when he had turned onto the state highway, he could see no tail lamps for miles.

He let up on the gas pedal while considering what to do next, but Anderson snapped, "Don't lose them, dammit!"

"Which way did they go then?"

"Take the next left coming up here."

"How do you know?"

"I don't. Just go left!"

A rough secondary road veered off the state highway. Ward recalled that it meandered southeast along a sluggish stream and that a score of farm and logging traces branched off it.

Again, no brake lamps were visible—the road

was mostly curves and its straight sections were few and far between.

"We shoulda tailed the kid," Anderson repeated.

"Do you think they saw us?"

"Christ, you have to be in the damned ballpark for them to see you!"

Ward took the bends fast and wide, trusting that no one was coming from the opposite direction. "I don't think they went this way."

"Keep going, now. Even if they kept to the highway, we'd never catch them now."

"Did you make the plates on the pickup?"

Anderson just laughed. But then he said, "Stop."

Ward hit the brakes so forcefully both Anderson and he slid forward on the seat. "What do you see?"

"Back up a mite."

Throwing the shift into reverse, Ward glanced down the darkened dirt lane that had apparently captured Anderson's attention. It looked no different than the other unmarked traces they had sped past.

"This is it," Anderson said.

"How the hell do you know that?"

"Look, dammit—those tire impressions!"

He was right: a vehicle had made the turn at a considerable speed, the tires spraying dirt beyond the shallow furrows they had dug out of the apron to the road.

"Slow now," Anderson said as Ward started down it, "and kill your lights." He held his head out the wide window, listening.

Ward clenched his lids for a few seconds so his eyes could more quickly adjust to the shadowy night. He opened them, and thought he could see something red glinting ahead. "What's that, Anderson?"

"Where?"

"Dead ahead."

"I don't see—" Anderson paused, then said with excitement in his voice for the first time, "That's the truck, Boss. We got them. Park here and we'll hoof it."

Both men got out without latching their doors and betraying their presence with the noise.

Like Anderson, Ward was grasping a unlit flashlight in his left hand and his revolver in his right. His shoulder was now throbbing, and inwardly he railed against his mind for invoking this false pain, this visceral memory of pain. It was keeping him from completely giving his attention to the job.

Something winged over the road, giving him a start.

An owl maybe.

The moon was still low enough in the east for it to be obscured by the trees, and its light was diffuse and of no help in illuminating the interior of the pickup's cab. Just when Ward thought he could discern the silhouette of a head, the vision dematerialized.

Anderson hand-signaled Ward to take driver's door, which was ajar. He would take the passenger side.

With an exaggerated nod Ward agreed.

Inching up to the GMC in concert with Anderson, he hooked the toe of his shoe inside the door and kicked it open.

Both flashlights clicked on in nearly the same instant.

Ward peered down over the sights of his revolver into the empty cab. Anderson thought first to check the bed of the truck, once again shaming Ward that he had failed to realize all the possibilities.

They turned off their flashlights and stood in the silence.

Then Ward caught a faint susurration of voices. Anderson failed to pick it up, for he was walking over to Ward as if for a conference when the young agent had to tell him in a whisper: "Across this little creek here—voices."

"You sure?"

"Absolutely."

Anderson led the way through the partial darkness, down a grassy slope to a tiny footbridge that delivered them onto the edge of a cotton field. The voices seemed to be coming from a gin house across the field.

Anderson and he were sifting through the knee-high plants as quietly as they could when a scream halted them. It went on and on, hysterically.

"Jesus," Ward said, sprinting forward, thrashing through the cotton.

Anderson was right behind him, urging him to slow down a bit, to be aware of an ambush. But Ward didn't care: he wanted only to answer that scream.

The gin house was farther than it had looked from the small creek, and it was at least a minute before Ward burst through the door and trained his flashlight beam on the youth, who was groveling in a pile of rotten burlap, his trousers pulled down around his shins.

"What is it?!" he cried over the Negro's screaming. "Where are you hurt?"

The youth drew his bloody, trembling hands away from his groin, and Ward bellowed. "Oh God!"

Anderson hobbled inside, his revolver and light held before him. Then, through the swirling motes of dust stirred up by the agonized youth, he too saw what had happened.

Rupert Anderson made a sound as if he himself had been cut.

She would rise from the couch at quarter to midnight and turn off the television. In the dwindling minutes before he arrived home for his midshift meal, she would savor a crème de menthe while standing at the sink, smoking. It was the only variety of spirits that she drank. Then she would carefully rinse her mouth, for she had failed to do so once and he'd pointed out in disgust that her teeth were still green.

Sighing, she opened the refrigerator and recoiled slightly from an unexpected mustiness. What was spoiling now?

Its discovery could wait until morning.

She decided on a ham sandwich for him. That was the safest choice, and she really didn't know what she would do if he started at her tonight. All the old resentments, safely stored these past years with her mother's lace doilies in her cedar hope chest, had been released. And by what?

The front screen door slammed shut.

"Clinton, is that you, now?" she asked, wondering why she bothered to ask what was only obvious.

"I don't have long," he groused, sweeping into the kitchen, bringing a stale tobacco smell with him. His leather gear creaked as he sat at the table.

"Is something going on?"

"Nothing that won't come out in the wash." A

pfft noise followed his words: a can of beer and an opener had been awaiting him on the table. "You about ready there?"

She tore a big leaf of her homegrown lettuce into a square that would fit the bread. "Yes. I hope you don't mind a ham sandwich."

His silence said for him that he had no objection.

She laid the plate before him, and he started chewing immediately, his eyes glazed as they bore sightlessly through and beyond her. Something had indeed happened tonight—his glassy look told her so. He worried a lot after he had done something that could never be reversed, and for that reason alone she believed him to be a weak man.

"You need a fresh shirt tonight, Clint?" Sometimes he was so sweat-soaked he changed mid-shift.

"Nope, been in the office with Ray all evening. He had the cooler going."

She despised that cooler, if only because he refused to buy one for the house when more and more folks were getting them from Sears Roebuck. His daddy, before he'd died six years ago, had mentioned once that refrigerated air made a man weak, took his legs away from him if he had to defend himself with his fists on a hot day. That had been enough to turn Clinton away from any idea of buying an air conditioner; what his daddy said was forever gospel. Of course, his daddy's words of wisdom didn't keep him from enjoying the cooler down at the station.

"Hell," he said out of the blue, "I got no time to dawdle." He scooted back his chair to rise, leaving two long scuffs on the linoleum she'd just waxed.

"You be careful, Clint," she said, her usual farewell as he departed again for work.

"Always do, babe."

And then he was gone. He had taken only a couple of bites of his sandwich.

It was not her habit, but tonight she had a second glass of the sweet green liquid. Smiling, feeling more wicked than she could remember, she tossed the partly eaten sandwich in the trash under the sink.

10

It unnerved Ward more than anything: how Anderson had not said a word since returning to the gin house other than to mumble that the men had eventually doubled back and escaped in their GMC pickup. Ward thought to himself that Anderson and he should have disabled the truck, perhaps pocketed the distributor cap, before venturing across the cotton field.

But meanwhile, he had stemmed the Negro's ghastly flow of blood with direct pressure, enough so that he could be safely moved. Yet the youth refused to be taken to the hospital in town. The prospect positively terrified him.

"But why?" Ward asked.

"Please just take me home, suh." He had just stopped vomiting, and his face was ashen in the glow of the flashlight.

"We'll make sure you get proper treatment."

"They's a colored doctor for me."

And so they drove him home, a weathered wooden shack in the small Negro section of town. Silently he embraced his mother, then collapsed in her arms.

Ward stayed with them while Anderson went for the doctor.

At first the old woman seemed stunned, yet in full command of herself. She even introduced herself as Mrs. Walker and explained that her son's name was Obie. But then she abruptly began wailing. And her wail was nearly as disquieting as her son's screams had been. But after a while, with the help of a neighbor woman who'd been drawn by her anguished cries, she settled down into weeping—and casting hateful looks in Ward's direction.

He wasn't sure if she understood that Anderson and he had not been among the men who had castrated her son. Perhaps a lifetime of abuses, big and small, had eroded her ability to make such distinctions.

The Plymouth Fury returned, and the Negro doctor hurried from it even before Anderson had braked to a crunching stop in the dooryard, which was paved with cinders.

"Where is he?" the doctor asked, rushing past Ward without waiting for his reply. Catching sight of the physician, the old woman began wailing again.

Anderson was leaning against the Fury's grill with his arms splayed back against the hood. His chin was resting on his tie, which he'd loosened.

Feeling exhausted and slightly shaky himself, Ward joined him. "How're you doing?" he asked.

Anderson nodded as if to say that he was all right, but he still looked ill. Ward supposed that he did, too.

After an hour of saying little, of tracking the crescent of moon across the night sky, they adjourned to the inside of the Plymouth and tried to doze. Ward finally did an hour or so later, for he dreamed of a high school lunchroom, of blood smeared across young, antagonistic faces.

When the doctor's footfalls on the porch awakened him, he saw the eastern horizon was a rich pink. He nudged Anderson. "Morning."

"Morning." Although wide-eyed, Anderson remained slumped inside the car as Ward got out.

He stole a quick stretch before crossing the cindery yard to the doctor. "Is he going to make it, sir?"

"You mean, is he going to live? Sure," the man said wearily. "But making it's entirely a different thing, now isn't it?"

"I suppose, Doctor. Can he talk right now?"

"Yes, but he's not going to."

"Why's that?"

"His mother's laid down the law—no talking to you."

"We need his help."

"He needs to live."

"Don't you see? There's been a violation of federal law here. We believe that someone acting under color of law made it possible for him to be subjected to this. See, that's covered by Section Two-forty-two, Title Eighteen, U.S. Code—and with his help we can get a conviction on that section."

"And who can you convict, Mr. Agent?"

"Those responsible for this."

"Every last one of the bastards?"

"Well, at least the principals."

"Ah," the doctor said knowingly. "Having some small acquaintanceship with the law, I'm asking myself what will become of the accessories to this violation."

Ward had no answer.

"I think Mrs. Walker's advice to her son is well considered, Mr. Agent. Why, just last evening I saw your director on television. Mr. Hoover was explaining to the press how his agency is an investigative one, not a police one, and that it's up to the Mississippi authorities to protect those who have been threatened by the kluckers." The doctor smiled bitterly. "He was extraordinarily careful to make the distinction between federal and state responsibilities. Unfortunately, I fear that distinction would be lost on the Walkers this morning."

Ward ran his hand through his hair. He felt like yanking it. "When in the name of God are we going to get some cooperation around here?" he exploded, immediately sorry that he had done so.

"When you can prevent the sort of thing that happened to this boy last night, Mr. Agent." The doctor regarded the sun, which had just begun to burgeon through the pinkish haze in the east. "Well, night is done, and all monsters are returned to their dens. I believe it's now safe for me to walk home."

"We'll drive you."

"No, thank you." With that, the doctor started down the lane, the weight of his black bag making his right arm seem a bit longer than his left.

Ward realized that Anderson was standing beside him, deeply silent as before.

"I swear this is the pattern," Ward mused out loud. "This is how it happened on June 21. Clinton Pell made his traffic stop on the boys at three that afternoon. He held them in a cell until he could make his phone calls and get his Klan friends organized. Even kluckers have jobs and dinner hours to think of. He released the kids at ten-thirty and went home whistling to himself. By that time his buddies were ready and waiting."

"No," Anderson said, his voice a rasp. "Pell rode with them that night. I'm sure of it."

Ward had never imagined that he might miss Anderson's smile. But he did. "You still have that pint of bourbon in your room?"

He nodded distantly.

"Let's see if we can kill it before breakfast."

"You're on." Finally, Rupert Anderson smiled a little.

"What's with the projection booth?" Anderson asked Ward later that morning, finding him on the mezzanine.

"We're setting up an interrogation room." The young agent said it so gleefully Anderson wondered if this had been the first time he'd ever mixed whiskey and fried eggs together. But then Ward lowered his voice: "Lucky break came in about an hour ago from Washington. Well," he corrected himself, "I shouldn't say lucky. We worked our asses off on this one."

"One what?"

"I had Byrd secretly take some snapshots of all the players in town here. Watching these Klan rally films gave me the idea."

"Whoa—what idea?"

"To compare the mugs of these locals against the faces in films. The photo-lab guys have been working around the clock ever since I shipped them our rogues' gallery. You know, going through the sixteen-millimeter reels frame by frame." Ward beamed. "The long and the short of it is that the Washington technicians came up with a lovely surprise we flat missed,

"We?"

"You and me, Mr. Anderson. We watched the very same film, and it went right over our heads."

Anderson was about to ask again what Ward was talking about when the lobby doors parted and two men barreled in, side by side. One of them was Deputy Clinton Pell, decked out in what were probably his going-to-church clothes. Flanking him was a soft little man in blue-and-white seersucker who just had to be an attorney. He was grinning like it was his first morning in heaven.

"This way please, gentlemen," Ward called down to them hospitably.

Pell and the little man started up the carpeted stairs, taking them two at a time.

"Good morning," Ward further greeted them, but only the attorney returned a hello. Of course, a Delta lawyer would be cordial to Lucifer himself. And why not? Anderson asked himself, feeling better than he had in days. They probably belonged to the same fraternal organizations.

Ward motioned for Anderson to join them inside the booth, where a long table and several chairs had been arranged to accommodate the two opposing sides. The FBI team, consisting of three attorney-agents and a stenographer, were already in place.

Anderson took a stool in the corner, but Ward sat directly across from Pell, who kept his eyes downcast as he lit up a Pall Mall. The shoulders of his dark jacket were peppered with dandruff.

The attorney squared his crimson bow tie before snapping open his briefcase. "I am sincerely hoping, gentlemen," he began prattling, "that these here proceedings—whatever they might properly be called—will be sufficiently brief for my friend and client"—significantly, he removed a new-looking copy of Title 18 of the U.S. Code from his case and set it before him on the table—"Mr. Pell to make work on time. His is a small law-enforcement department, lacking the considerable manpower of yours, and his absence will result in a most dire inconvenience to the public safety."

"We wouldn't want that, sir," Ward said, sounding amused. The Bureau's stenographer, brought in this morning from the new field office in Jackson, looked at him to ask if she should start recording. He nodded for her to do so, to which Anderson silently agreed: a lawyer like this spewed the same bullshit whether on or off the record.

"Are you Clinton Pell?"

The deputy dipped his head once, which then required Ward to repeat the question.

"I am Clinton Pell," he sighed.

At this point Ward advised the deputy of his constitutional rights, told him that whatever he said might be used against his interests in a court of law, particularly a federal court.

Anderson wanted to groan: nobody, including the august members of the United States Supreme Court, had come to terms with what precisely those rights were, and he was sure that Ward had only succeeded in opening a huge can of worms.

This was proved a moment later when Pell's attorney leaned forward and asked him as if his mouth were full of hot okra: "Is my client to infer from this admonition that he's in your custody?"

Ward turned to the attorney-agent on his right, who whispered in his ear. "Mr. Pell is not to consider himself in our custody."

"Then we can safely assume that he is not under arrest?"

"Yes, sir, he is not under arrest."

Anderson pinched the bridge of his nose with his fingers. On general principle, he seldom listened to the advice of an attorney-agent. There were a good number of them, law school graduates who'd passed the bar only to forgo a life of wealth and prestige in order to become G-men, doing what an ignoramus like Roop Anderson did passably well without benefit of several years of costly higher education. For this reason alone he suspected their common sense.

But whether or not Ward and his team of legal eagles realized it, this wily backwoods lawyer had already set his trap for them. Now he was only waiting for the right moment in which to spring it.

"Excellent, gentlemen," he said amiably. "For it was my client's and my understanding that this would simply be an interview to facilitate an investigation being conducted by your agency into the disappearance of three young men."

"This is correct," Ward agreed too quickly to suit one of the attorney-agents, who motioned for him to bend his way for a quick whisper. When Ward sat straight again, he looked as if his hand had just been slapped with a ruler.

Anderson asked himself why they hadn't better prepared themselves for this dog-and-pony show. The only way to get anything out of Clinton Pell was to scare it out of him, and the deputy seemed far from frightened as he smirked around the filter of his Pall Mall.

"Mr. Pell," Ward forged ahead, "On the night of June 21, did you knowingly release three volunteers of the Voter Education Project of the Council of Federated Organizations into the hands of the Ku Klux Klan?"

The deputy plucked the cigarette from his lips and said defiantly, "No."

"Do you know what I mean when I say Ku Klux Klan?"

For an instant Pell's eyes flickered back and forth in confusion. "Sure."

"Do you also know what I mean when I say 'klavern'?"

"Who the hell around here don't?" Pell gave his lawyer an uneasy sideward smile, and Anderson found himself encouraged by it. Inadvertently maybe, Ward had touched a nerve, and now—with a little savvy—he might find a button as well.

"Will you agree that the president of a Klan klavern is commonly called its 'Grand Cyclops'?"

"I suppose."

"Yes or no, Mr. Pell, please."

"Excuse me, gentlemen," the lawyer said, grinning again. "But I fail to see the pertinence of this information—"

"Believe me, sir," Ward interrupted, "but this information is extremely pertinent to our investigation, and we would greatly appreciate the cooperation of your client in corroborating it."

The lawyer decided to back off for the moment. "Very well," he said, catching Pell's bewildered expression, "if your stenographer might reread the question for my client's benefit.

She did so, and the deputy said, "Yes, I've heard that's what they call their president. So what?"

"And are you, in fact, the Grand Cyclops of the Southwest Mississippi Klavern of the White Knights of the Ku Klux Klan?"

Pell held Ward's eyes for a long moment. "No."

"Are you presently or have you ever been a member of the White Knights of the Ku Klux Klan?"

"No."

"Are you presently or have you ever been a member of any division of the Ku Klux Klan?"

Pell's lawyer had been looking for an opening and finally found it: "Objection, my client has already answered that he's not a member of the Klan."

"This is just an interview, sir," Ward said. "There's really no need to be so formal."

"Isn't there, sir? This 'interview' has suddenly turned so accusatory I have begun to question your motives in requesting my client's presence. Perhaps," he said drolly, "your admonition of rights was in order and my client is indeed under federal arrest."

"Again, he is not in our custody."

Pell then revealed that he had at least a cursory understanding of the issues at hand. "Well, if this is just an interview, I guess I don't have to stay here, do I?"

The FBI people stared at him as he came to his feet. Anderson shook his head.

"I got work to do." Pell leered at Ward. "I guess you do, too, hah?"

"And you can be sure we'll do it, too. By the way, you might be interested in this." The young agent skidded an eight-by-ten still across the table to Pell. It was of him dressed in the robes of a grand cyclops of White Knights of the Ku Klux Klan.

Surprisingly, the deputy kept a poker face as he examined the photograph. "Who's this supposed to be?" he finally said, flinging it back at Ward.

Pell's attorney followed him out, pausing only to say over his shoulder, "Morning, gentlemen, ma'am."

"Y'all get enough to indict me," the deputy shouted from mezzanine, "you know where to find me!" Then his lawyer could be heard shushing him.

Ward conferred with the attorney-agents for a few moments more, then ambled across the projection booth to Anderson, who was still perched on the stool.

"What do you think?" he asked, yawning.

Anderson thought that for all this legal frou-frou, nothing more had been learned than what had already surmised from the Pell's wedding picture—that the deputy was a klucker from the word go. But he decided that now was not the moment in which to goad Ward. "How'd you find out he was grand cyclops to the klavern here?"

"An informant sang after we showed him the photo."

"Somebody inside the Klan?" Anderson asked hopefully.

"No, afraid not."

"Then how'd he know for sure Pell is cyclops? The kluckers I used to know would rather swallow their tongues than blab about their leadership."

"The informant doesn't know for sure, at least for testimony purposes. But at least it's one more thread."

We're dancing at the end of too many strings, Anderson said inwardly, *what we need are some goddamned leads.* But he nodded as if he agreed with Ward and started for the door; the projection booth had grown stuffy. "Too bad we didn't do this little gig in front of a federal grand jury."

"Why's that?"

"We coulda nailed Pell's ass for perjury."

"We thought of that," Ward said somewhat defensively. "But we didn't feel we had enough to present to the jury. Simply belonging to the Klan isn't a crime."

"Exactly."

Ward seemed on the verge of realizing that he'd just admitted the futility of the interview when his and Anderson's attention was drawn to the front doors of the theater. Pell, flanked now by both his lawyer and Sheriff Stuckey, had stepped through them into a maelstrom of reporters, whose shouted questions were loud enough to carry through the glass:

"Is it true you're about to be indicted?"

Pell threw up his forearm against a frenzy of flashbulbs.

"Or are you cooperating with the investigation?"

"Yeah, Deputy, are you turning state's evidence in hope of some kind of deal?"

"Boys, boys!" Raymond Stuckey cried in that brittle affability he had now adopted in all brushes with the media. "How 'bout letting us pass through now? A fella could use Moses to get through y'all!"

"Sheriff, does the FBI have evidence that your office was involved in the homicides?"

"What homicides?" Stuckey spun on the newsman, dropping the mask of affability even though shutters were still clicking on all sides of him and beyond the reporters stood echelons of townies, attracted to the shade of the marquee by all the excitement. "Just what homicides you talking about there, mister?"

Anderson laughed under his breath: the reporter had enough moxie to stand his ground; he'd probably tangled with bigger fish in official-dom. "The homicides being investigated by the

FBI—and allegedly an investigation being obstructed by you and your deputy."

But the reporter had probably never tangled with the likes of Frank Bailey, who was inching up behind him with a murderous look on the puttylike flesh of his face.

"We're cooperating just like we been all along!" Stuckey was yelling when Bailey wound back his fist and clobbered the reporter from behind, spilling him into the sheriff, who pushed him aside as if he were a leper. "No!" he went on strangely, giving the impression that he was the only person in the throng who had not seen Bailey coldcock the newsman. "There's not one itty bit of evidence against—!"

"You point that thing at me one more time, and I'll shove up your goddamn ass!" Frank Bailey roared at a television cameraman.

This fellow had the good sense to withdraw, although still shooting as he backed his way out of the crowd. Another cracker popped him on the ear, hard, but he didn't go down.

Ward started down the stairs toward the melee, but Anderson snagged him by the sleeve. "Whoa, this is definitely a local law-enforcement matter."

"It's a godammned riot on our doorstep!"

"Isn't the first time, Mr. Ward. And it won't be the last." Anderson was laughing—in admiration, almost. "You're aching to get down there and mix it up a little, aren't you?"

Ward gave a sheepish hike of his shoulders. "Don't get sanctimonious with me, Mr. Anderson."

"Oh, I'm not. I'm just recommending you throw your punches when nobody's looking. Especially when no news media is looking."

At that moment Lyle Tilman charged through

the doors and up the stairs, one of his shirt collars sticking out. "Mr. Ward! This is getting to be about as much as we can take. I cannot register my complaints more strongly to you!"

"Mr. Mayor?"

"I resent your public harassment of our most trusted law-enforcement officials. You've made every effort to smear them with these disappearances, but your damned innuendos are not evidence that they are connected in any way to any crime!"

"We're just trying to get to the truth, sir," Ward said with an innocent tone of voice Anderson respected for its complete lack of sincerity. Ward was learning a thing or two about dealing with Southern politicians. "We're accusing no one at this point. And if the press makes groundless assumptions about our activities, it's frustrating for us, too."

"Any jackass can point fingers, Ward. But pointing ain't proof. And down here us cotton choppers are still naive enough to believe in democracy. We know our rights under the law."

"Oh, you know things, all right," Anderson said quietly, stripping the foil off a fresh stick of Beaman's Spearmint.

"What was that?" Tilman demanded, sniffing an insult.

"I was just saying, Mayor, that I'd bet a cotton-chopping dollar that you do indeed know things."

"Listen here, Anderson, after that stunt at the social club, you're so far up my nose I'm feeling your boots on my chin! And I'm telling you both—a couple crazies in bed sheets going around scaring the nigras ain't the goddamn fault of the entire state of Mississippi!"

"And I'm telling you, Tilman," Ward said evenly,

"there's three dead kids out there somewhere and people in this town somewhere who know how it happened. And we're staying here until those people decide that it's in their best interests to talk. So you better get used to us being around."

"And used to my boots tapping on your chin," Anderson added.

Lyle Tilman turned on his heel and rushed out the doors again, only to be besieged by several microphones. But he made no attempt to bat them away, as Stuckey and Pell had during their final rush for their cruiser. "Goddamn right I got a statement!" he bellowed.

"You know," Ward said, "for a minute there it sounded like we were on the same side.'"

But Anderson said nothing. He simply chewed his gum and studied his hands, which he'd folded over the grimy brass railing.

The late afternoon sky was overcast, and Mrs. Pell sensed the mist worming up from the lowlands to the west, bringing with it the steamy mustiness of the river. She parked beside her small house, lifted the two grocery bags from the floor of the rear bench seat, only to set them down a moment later on the porch steps so she could scratch a chigger bite on her elbow.

"It's not gonna rain for all this humidity, don't you know, now," her neighbor called out from her kitchen window. The woman's face seemed ghostly in the dimness behind the screen.

"Pity, ain't it, Margaret?" Mrs. Pell gave a dilatory reply, for she'd just noticed a black Dodge Polara parked at the end of the street.

"You all right, honey?"

"Certainly," she said in the same remote tone of voice. "Do I look peaked or something?"

"Just tired."

"That I am." She picked up her bags, but paused with her hand on the screen door latch. Down the street he had gotten out of the Dodge and was standing behind the open door expectantly, as if waiting for her to beckon him. She could imagine the sad smile he was probably wearing.

"There you go again, honey," her neighbor said over the sound of her running taps. "You sure you shouldn't go inside and lie down a spell?"

"Maybe I should, Margaret."

"You let me know if you need anything."

"I will. Thanks."

And suddenly she couldn't find her house key quickly enough. It seemed forever before she was safely inside with the security bolt engaged behind her. *But engaged against what?* she asked herself, feeling weepy all of a sudden. She leaned against the door and closed her eyes tightly to keep the tears from coming. "Sweet Jesus, save me from this . . . I'm not strong enough for this . . ."

Ten minutes later, when she'd worked up the nerve to glance outside, the Dodge was gone. But, as anticipated, the mist had sifted in from the lowlands, enveloping the houses and trees of the neighborhood in its sultry arms.

11

Going outside was better in summer than in winter. All but the biggest stars had faded when he picked through the straw of the coop for eggs. In summer Willie had only his own sleepiness to deal with, but in winter there was the cold, and it could seem most awful on those dawns when frost was clinging to the grass and making the tips of the honeysuckle vines look like they'd been burned. Sometimes his chilly fingers found it almost impossible to close around the eggs, unless the hen had been sitting on them right before he slipped through the chicken-wire door—some of those eggs seemed deliciously warm in his hands.

Some of the folks had lived up North and always said that a Mississippi winter was nothing compared to a northern one. And they threw in stories about this or that farmer up North getting lost between his dooryard and the barn in a terrible blizzard, wandering blind out in his fields until he dropped dead from the cold; or about some little kid resting his tongue on an icy rail and getting it stuck fast until a train come along and took his head off at the neck. Because of this latter story, Willie had never licked a rail, nor would he ever do so, regardless of the weather.

He went into the coop and began carefully gathering the few eggs there were this morning in an old tin pot. He was thinking about a train thundering down on some poor kid with his tongue stuck when he heard tires on the cinder-paved road.

It was so unusual enough to hear a car in the neighborhood this early, he went to the wire-covered window at the back of the coop and looked out on the road, which was less than ten feet away. For several moments he saw nothing. But that was only because the pickup truck was running without lights through the bluish dawn gloom. As it crept past the coop, the lower half of the truck was hidden by the honeysuckle vines that were heaped over the old fence line, but the upper half—including the cab—was plain for him to see.

Four white men were jammed in the seat, their pale faces catching what little light there was.

Willie knew the four men.

The pickup continued down the cindery road, then braked in front of Obie Walker's house. The white man sitting at the passenger window flung something that broke and made a tinkling sound against Obie's porch. A big gush of orange flame shot up and curled around the overhang. The living room window exploded like it'd been taken out with buckshot, and then smoke started drifting across the road.

The driver of the truck made a U-turn and drove past the coop again, slowly as he pleased, like he'd just delivered the mail. Willie ducked below the windowsill and waited in a crouch until he couldn't hear the tires anymore.

Then he bolted from the coop and ran for his house. "Mama! Mama! Somebody threw something on Obie's porch!"

She met him at the kitchen door, wiping the flour off her hands into her apron. Then, without Willie having to say anything more, her eyes got wild as they stopped on Obie's house. The front of it was all flames, and their crackling was loud enough to make all the neighborhood dogs start barking.

His mother began gazing from house to house, maybe wondering which grown man to send Willie after.

But then Obie and his mother hurried out the back of their fiery house, choking on the smoke but otherwise unharmed. Obie was walking stiff-legged, and Willie supposed this had something to do with the bad thing that had happened to him, something Willie didn't quite understand, but understood enough to make no mention of it in public.

"Obie!" he cried.

But Obie Walker just stood beside his mama, watching their house melt up into the sky. The sun was touching the very top of the pall.

Ward and Anderson met John Byrd at the scene. The special agent had been there since the tardy arrival of the fire trucks, and Ward immediately took him aside. "Any idea what the accelerant was?"

"Probably kerosene, Mr. Ward. The front of the place still smells like kerosene."

"Where are the Walkers?"

"Gone even before I got here."

"Any witnesses?" Ward asked, trying not to sound too desperate.

"None who'll talk to us, sir."

"Dammit!"

Anderson, who had been stubbing through the debris with the toe of his shoe, glanced up. "What's the problem?"

"I want the entire area covered," Ward said so all the agents present could hear. "Someone must have seen something. A house isn't torched in the middle of a neighborhood without—"

"But they won't talk to us, sir," Byrd butted in.

For the first time in memory, Ward found himself actually disliking the man. "Get going, Mr. Byrd. If they won't talk, shake it out of them."

Byrd was wide-eyed. "Shake it out of them?"

"That's right."

"I'm not sure I understand your instructions, sir."

Ward spun away from him and nearly bumped chests with Anderson, who dropped the stick of spearmint he'd been preparing to pop in his mouth.

"Whoa, Mr. Ward," he said quietly, picking up his gum and brushing the cinder dust off it. "Mr. Byrd's got a point. You shake martinis, not people."

"Then what do you suggest, Mr. Anderson? Forget this case and have an early lunch?"

"Not at all." He began chewing thoughtfully.

Your temper, Ward reminded himself. "I'm listening, Mr. Anderson."

"There is somebody who'll talk to us. Hell, he's done everything but rent a billboard to tell us so."

"Who?"

"I figure the less we speak his name the better. Let's just drop by his place, and make sure to park around back."

"Then, let's go," Ward said, his voice still full of irritation. On the way to the Dodge he leveled his forefinger at Byrd. "By the time I return, I want this fire's point of origin located."

"Yes, sir."

"And the accelerant not probably determined but definitely determined. I don't care if you have to call in one of the lab people from the new Jackson office. In fact, do call him in. That's what he's here for."

"Yes, sir."

"You drive," Ward snapped at Anderson. Then, slamming the passenger front door, he groaned with frustration, "Jesus, whatever we touch around here goes up in flames!"

"Mr. Ward . . ."

"What?"

"You know, Mr. Byrd isn't responsible for what happened here. And neither are you."

Ward stared at him quizzically, then looked forward again. "It'd be nice to believe that."

Four hours later, they were sitting in Vertis Williams's shabby parlor, each of them balancing a plate of chocolate cake on one knee and a tumbler of lemonade on the other. Mrs. Williams, who had prepared these treats, had yet to appear. And early in their visit, Vertis, his head still bandaged, had withdrawn to a corner of the room, where he sat silently—except for an occasional cough—in a threadbare wingback chair as if keeping a death vigil on a relative.

On behalf of the FBI men, young Aaron Williams was calmly interviewing a boy half his age named Willie, who had shyly appeared in the last

thirty minutes and was still so nervous he'd refused the offer of cake and lemonade.

"And then what happened, Willie?" Aaron asked.
"They go speeding off in the truck?"

"No, they go away real slow."

"What kind of truck you say?"

"I didn't, Aaron."

"What was it?"

"I don't know. I don't know trucks real good."

"What color was it?"

"Old color."

"Dark or light?"

"Dark, I guess."

"Good, Willie. You're doing fine."

Ward made a mental note to mail Aaron Williams a GS application in about ten years: so far
he had solicited more information from the frightened boy in ten minutes than Anderson and he
had in twenty.

"What about the four white men in the truck,
Willie?"

His eyes stopped shifting in his small face.

"It's okay to be scared," Aaron said. "I was scared
when them night riders waited for us on the road.
I was real scared when I got kicked by Lester
Cownes the way I did."

But Willie continued to say nothing.

"You know the men, don't you, Willie?"

A barely perceptible nod.

"You know all four?"

"Yes, but . . ." Fear choked off his words, and
for an instant Ward wanted to terminate the interview and leave the house. The boy looked that
pathetic, sitting so small on the couch with his
hands tucked between skinny thighs. "I got to
look at them if'n they go to jail?"

Aaron glanced at Ward. It was a moment before the agent realized that Willie was asking if he'd have to confront and identify the suspects. "Yes, I'm afraid that—"

"I got an idea," Anderson said cheerfully, setting his cake and lemonade on the braided rug. "Aaron, does your mama have a big paper sack we can use?"

Appearing confused, Aaron nevertheless rose. "I'll check."

"Paper sack saved me many a time," Anderson went on. "Why, if it hadn't been for paper sacks, I'd never got any gals to go out with me in high school."

For the first time Vertis chuckled. But it seemed to hurt his head, so he stopped.

"We got no sack, but how's this?" Aaron asked, returning. He was holding a small pasteboard box.

"That should do just dandy." Accepting it from the youth, Anderson then cut two slits for eye holes with his pocket knife. "There, now, try this on for size, Willie." He smiled. "Well, it ain't the smartest in haberdashery, but it'll do fine for a little spin around town."

"The defendants will rise."

One thing could be said about Mississippi justice, Anderson thought to himself as he gazed around at the all too familiar ambience of burnished mahogany and middle-aged Southern men in summer-weight suits, it could be as swift as Mississippi sunsets. Particularly with the entire civilized world staring down the collar of this flyspeck burg through the lens of a television camera. It had been only ten days since little Willie, cowering in the backseat of the Dodge Polara, had suddenly piped up: "They's one of them, Mr. Anderson. Him in front of the feed store." Ward had looked triumphant then and also when he had succeeded in having the trial moved to another county, but Anderson had thought any celebration premature.

"In this country," the judge intoned, peering gravely over the tops of his bifocals at the four yahoos who'd torched Obie Walker's house to the ground, "a man's home is his castle. That's one of the cherished principles by which this community survives. And you men have done violence to that principle."

And violence to Hollis Johnson, Anderson mused, whom you four rednecks most likely kidnapped and beat within an inch of his life. It had sorely disappointed Ward that he'd been unable to turn one of the defendants against the others, but Anderson had not entertained such a frail hope: the FBI, despite the hoopla of establishing a new field office in Jackson, was temporary; the Klan was forever, and none of these hulking boys was about to forget it.

"But I want you to understand that the court appreciates the fact that crimes you have committed have been, to some extent at least, mitigated by outside influences."

The court was filled with murmuring, especially from the press, and Ward looked positively stupefied before he hung his head in resignation. He was smart enough to sense what was coming.

And come it did:

"Outsiders have been flooding into your community, and they have been—insofar as some of them are considered, at least—men and women of low morality and licentious views. Frankly, a goodly number of them are unhygienic—"

Anderson chuckled under his breath, although the bailiff apparently heard it, for he censured him with a hard glance.

"And let it be known that I have absolutely no doubt in my mind that the presence of these people has provoked behavior in the local population that is foreign to the morals of this community. I say that as a man who has sat on this bench for twenty-three years now—"

"Then it's about time he stood up for a spell," Anderson whispered to Ward. "I think he's pinched off the flow of blood to his brain."

But the young agent was too distraught to smile. He had begun to slowly wag his head, drunkenly almost.

"So the court understands—without condoning them, mind you—that the crimes to which you men have pled nolo contendere were to some extent excited by these outside influences." The judge glowered at the press seats: "For the benefit of the fourth estate, whose interest in these proceedings has been excessive to say the least, I will explain that a plea of nolo contendere is not the same as a plea of guilty. It is derived, of course, from the Latin, meaning: 'I wish not to contend.' And, in a nutshell, it means that the defendant, without admitting guilt, subjects himself to criminal conviction—and without denying himself the opportunity to challenge the truth of those charges in a collateral proceeding."

By collateral proceedings, the judge was referring to federal prosecution. By making a plea in this manner, the defendants were providing themselves with a dodge in case the U.S. attorney decided to have a whack at them. Anderson had anticipated that their lawyers would talk them into

doing precisely this, even though it was the con-
sensus of the national legal community that the
U.S. Justice Department did not have a strong
enough case to warrant a horrendous states'-rights
battle with Mississippi, one that might appear to
verify the Klan's outlandish claim that Washington was just two steps away from clamping federal
control on Jackson, enforced of course by a military occupation.

Whatever, it was over: another dry well of a
lead, another aborted effort at getting a local in-
sider to tattle on the White Knights. Once again it
hit him—why he had walked away from his sheriff's
office when he'd been a shoo-in for at least another term. Why he had turned his back on his
troubled origins, despite his love for this country,
its sensible pace of life.

With a knowing smile Anderson listened to the
culmination of this light opera that had contained
everything except an aria about how Mississippians
had unduly suffered at the seige of Vicksburg.

"So keeping all this in mind," the judge said to
the defendants with a hint of paternal benignity in
his eyes, as if the sheriff had caught them out on
the road in a convertible, swatting mailboxes off
their posts with a Louisville Slugger, "I am going
to make your punishment commensurate not only
to the crimes with which you have been charged,
but to the unsettled situation I have just described,
as well." He paused, probably just to establish a
momentous tone for what followed: "I sentence
you each to five years in the state penitentiary."

Ward began lean forward with happy disbelief
written all over his face. But before the young
agent could go completely delirious with self-
congratulation, Anderson gently restrained him

by grasping his forearm. He knew that the judge was not finished.

"But I am going to suspend those sentences in favor of a program of informal parole under my direct auspices." His gavel fell for the last time.

The newsmen bolted from their seats to wrangle for the single pay telephone in the corridor. For all intents and purposes, this had been an acquittal, and that is how they would report it to the world.

"Ten days and nights of work down the toilet," Ward said, his voice nearly a whisper.

"It was a helluva gamble. I told you that at the start, Mr. Ward."

"One we shouldn't have taken?"

"Maybe," Anderson said carefully. "But no use in crying over spilt milk now."

"No, I'm not going to cry over it." Ward came to his feet. "But I'm sure not going to fuck around with a local court again."

On the way out, Anderson looked up at the colored gallery: none of the Negroes had left their chairs.

He shrugged his apologies in their direction, but no one responded.

Anderson savored only one bourbon while alone in his motel room, for he trusted that the evening would not pass uninterrupted and later he would need a clear head. A lousy thing sometimes—a clear head. Gazing between his stocking feet, he watched the Jackson news, which was nothing but reactions pro and con to the trial.

Not wanting to face the gloating eyes of the townies, he had skipped supper, opting instead for a package of Twinkies, which he washed down with Jim Beam.

"These fellas have been acquitted by the high court of this jurisdiction," a tense-looking Raymond Stuckey was saying, the cheap black-and-white set turning his ordinarily pinkish face the color of bread mold. "So it's time we get things back to normal."

"But they were not acquitted, Sheriff," the reporter clarified. "The plea amounted to a—"

"Well, I'm not going to split hairs, son. I'll leave that to the legal profession."

Anderson pressed the extra pillow over his face, blotting out the TV's silvery light banding across the room. He had not caught sight of her in nine days now, which only meant that she was avoiding him. It hurt to think that she would do such a thing, but he supposed that he understood. What was he offering anyway? Just some pretty talk, if he dared call it that, and a bouquet of trumpet pitchers now and again. A woman needed a lot more than that, even a woman who was saddled with Clinton Pell for better or for worse.

Suddenly he threw the pillow aside.

The town fire siren was wailing.

"Here it comes," he murmured.

Less than a minute later his door was rattled by knocking.

"Enter," he said, not having bothered to lock it. Hell, the entire motel was now a Bureau garrison— Fort Hoover, the locals had nicknamed it.

John Byrd rushed inside and raised his voice over the undulating of the siren: "There's trouble in the Negro section, Mr. Anderson."

"No shit, friend."

"Mr. Ward wants you to come with him at once."

Anderson wearily swung his legs over the side of the bed and reached for his shoes, which were still warm to the touch. "Tell the boss I'm on my way to the car."

12

Given the modest size of the town, Ward could not imagine how this situation might develop into much of a riot. Over the past few years he had been rushed to a number of northern cities in civil convulsion and, of course, to both Oxford and Birmingham when their Negro rage had boiled over. Those had been bona fide riots with the smoky aura of war hanging around the tenements and fire-gutted business districts. But to this evening's disturbance he had decided not to overreact, particularly in light of the assertion Director Hoover was repeatedly making: that the FBI was an investigative and not a police agency.

Only two of them would respond; the rest of the agents would remain at the motel on standby. And those two agents would be Anderson and himself.

Anderson sat on the far end of the front seat, his knee propped on the dashboard in what might have been taken for insouciance except for the fact that he'd just unholstered his revolver and checked each of the six rounds in the cylinder. He had forgotten to wear his tie, but in light of the rush with which he'd been summoned, Ward decided not to mention the lapse in discipline.

"Have they called in the troopers?" Anderson asked.

"Yes." Ward tilted his wristwatch toward the dash lights. "About twenty minutes ago a dozen of them arrived from Jackson. More are enroute from outlying substations."

"What's burning?"

"A mom and pop grocery. Negro-owned."

"Well," Anderson said, "riots aren't famous for breeding rationality. What's Stuckey's plan? Clear and secure the area behind a line of troopers?"

"I have no idea what he intends." Through his rolled-down side window Ward caught a whiff of smoke, acrid and ominous. "He hasn't returned my call."

"Probably thinks you're ready to barge in and start calling the shots."

"Probably."

"Get a load of that." Anderson was pointing at the jail entrance to the courthouse, which was crowded with special deputy types in varying degrees of law-enforcement regalia. "Looks like old Raymond has called out the posse. I don't think there's been more diverse and antiquated firearms in one spot since the Battle of Concord."

It send a ripple through Ward's gut to see the heavily armed townsmen jawing with each other in high spirits. "What are their qualifications to perform riot duty?"

"The only one that counts hereabouts—they supported Ray Stuckey in the last election."

"Terrific."

"With any luck they'll shoot each other."

Ward left the square behind and within a few blacked-out blocks of white houses entered the Negro section, which began with the unpaved lane on which Obie Walker's home had stood and ended in the orange glow of the grocery at the southern limits of town. A Mississippi Highway Safety Patrol radio car was parked broadside in the middle of the street, its bubblegum machine spangling the needles of some nearby spruces, making them look like Christmas.

Ward pulled alongside the flashlight-waving trooper, who did everything but salute as he said, "I'm very sorry, sir, but for your own safety you can't go in there."

Absently he wondered if a Negro driver would get the same spiel, but then he simply flashed his Bureau identification before he said something untoward. "FBI, Officer."

"Oh, good evening."

"We'd like to talk with Sheriff Stuckey, if we can find him."

"Well, sir, he's about two blocks inside. But if I was you, I'd hike in. Any car that even remotely looks official has been getting stoned pretty bad."

"Any injuries so far?"

"Just colored."

Again Ward held his tongue. "Has a command post been set up?"

The trooper didn't look like he knew what a such a thing was. "Sheriff's about two blocks inside," he repeated himself.

South of them, a shotgun boomed twice.

"Pop goes the weasel," the trooper said with so little inflection Ward didn't know if it had been a joke.

"Yeah, pop goes the weasel. Thanks for the tip." He inched forward and parked on the grassy shoulder.

"Want me to tote along the scatter gun?" Anderson asked.

While Ward vacillated over letting him get the shotgun out of the trunk, headlamps glanced around the corner two blocks distant, and a moment later Stuckey's Lincoln Continental sped into view.

The windshield was covered with powdery-looking divots—rock damage. Catching sight of the two agents standing beside their Dodge, the sheriff braked hard, slewing to a stop beside them. He rolled down his side window so furiously Ward thought for a moment that he'd snapped off the handle, but the object in his fist proved only to be his cigar. "Where the hell you think you're going?"

"We were thinking of looking for you, Sheriff," Ward said.

"Well, you found me."

"We wanted to know if we could be of any assistance."

Stuckey laughed, but his laugh was somewhat feeble, like that of a man at the end of his rope. Gesturing with his cigar at the glow spreading over the southern end of his town, he said, "You already been more help than my office and a score of troopers can properly handle, Ward."

"Is the situation that bad?"

"Oh, it's bad, but not so bad Mississippians can't handle it. And if you go past this trooper here into nigger-town, I'll toss you both in my jail. That's a goddamn promise, Hoover boys."

"Is this still the part of the United States, Sheriff?"

Stuckey's eyes narrowed. "What the hell kind of smart-ass question is that?"

"Unless Mississippi has seceded again, which is highly unlikely, Special Agent Anderson and I will go where we see fit. Interfere with us, and I'll make sure you have a nice long stay at Marion Federal Penitentiary. That's a goddamn promise, Sheriff."

Stuckey glowered at him for several seconds, then accelerated back toward downtown, forced to sit at an angle in order to see through his demolished windshield.

"There," Anderson said approvingly, "that's how to talk to these old boys so you get yourself a smidgen of respect."

"You're a bad influence on me, Mr. Anderson."

"Somebody's gotta be, Mr. Ward. Ain't anything more insufferable in this whole wide world than a perfect human being."

The horses were nickering, but not in the way they ordinarily did. Then, even though he was inside the kitchen, Aaron Williams could hear their hooves thudding against the packed earth of the corral, a staccato beating that told him they were skittishly running this direction and that.

He parted the curtains above the galvanized steel sink, expecting to see nothing but blackness and stars on account of there being no yard light—they'd only gotten electricity two years ago.

But he did see something.

And it seemed so astonishing to watch flickers of yellow fire wriggling through the cracks around the big double doors of the barn he did nothing but gape at them for a few seconds, wondering how this was possible—but already sensing through his confusion that the ofays were behind it. His mind's eye put white faces out in the darkness, although he could see no men, only the shadows of the horses rippling across the dusty ground in front of the barn.

Then the lowing of the milk cow trapped inside her stall shook him out of this lassitude, and he ran for the parlor. "Papa!"

Vertis Williams met him in the hallway and clenched the boy's bony shoulders in his big hands.

"Papa!"

"Settle down . . . what?"

"Fire . . . our barn!"

Vertis started moving toward the kitchen door, which opened onto the back of the house, but suddenly he drew to a halt and turned toward his son. His face looked frightened but also strangely tender as he said, "Aaron, take your mama out the front way, you hear? Go through the trees. When you hit the road, keep going south. You understand? Don't go toward town—they's trouble there too."

Something in his father's eyes prevented Aaron from arguing, although he wanted very much to argue. He felt as if now was the last time he would ever see him, and from this realization sprang such a hollow, lonely feeling he wanted to beg his father to stay.

But he didn't.

Instead he went for his mother, who'd already been abed an hour. She seldom stayed up much past supper.

Bursting through the bedroom door, he was prepared to tell her that the barn was on fire. But then he saw that she already knew, for she was down on her knees, praying with her eyes tightly shut and her lips quivering.

"We got to go, Mama," he said, taking her hand.

Her gaunt face was most queer: in the time it

took him to grasp her hand, it had turned calm, although in an eerie sort of way with no apparent mindfulness of what was happening around them.

She didn't resist his tug and followed as if she were a lost child, content just to have somebody take her hand. She didn't say anything, and Aaron had a strong inkling she wouldn't say anything for hours, maybe even for days. Her own father had been lynched, Vertis had explained once, thereafter refusing to answer Aaron's questions about what had happened to the grandfather he'd never known or why his mother shied away from company.

In the hallway Vertis brushed past them on his rush to the kitchen again, snicking a pair of shells into his breach-loaded shotgun, the same fowling piece that had brought down countless blue geese. Aaron knew it wasn't good to think of things other than that which his father had commanded him to do, but he found himself longing for one of those misty winter mornings to come when together they'd hunker down in the blind they'd built along the edge of the swamp. He wanted this night to be spent and for it to be winter, with the land cool and moist. Bad things always seemed to happen in the heat of summer, and this had been the hottest summer in memory.

"Go now," Vertis said one last time, catching Aaron's eye and smiling a little as if everything was going to be all right.

He had often prayed that his father could be a braver man, for it shamed him how Vertis always turned away from trouble. But now that his prayer was being answered, maybe, he wished that his father would put down the twelve-gauge and run away with them.

Aaron had never been so mixed up.

Vertis swept the bandage off his head and chucked it in the corner behind the woodstove. Quietly he slipped out the back door in a crouch, like he did when he tried to catch geese on the ground.

Aaron pulled his mother out the front into the hot, still night in which the crickets and frogs refused to sing for some reason. A long, weedy slope awaited them before the safety of the woods, and he kept her moving, tugging her arm hard whenever she slowed or began to whimper. It was awful to behold her like this, scared into being a child again, but he had always sensed that something wasn't right about his mama, and now he *saw* that a night long ago like this one had done it to her.

They were almost to the trees when his father's voice echoed up the slope: "Who's there?!"

Aaron stopped to listen, and his mother collapsed into the thick prairie clover, weeping softly.

He waited for a white voice to answer his father's, but none came.

"If you there, you come out, you hear me!" Vertis went on.

Aaron had never heard him so packed with rage; he didn't even sound like the same man. It was scary how different his father sounded. He couldn't see him, even though the fire was creeping up the cedar shingles of the barn roof and casting a stark light all over the slight depression in which their farm stood.

"I ain't taking this horseshit no more!" Vertis cried, pointing the shotgun at the rectangular shadow tossed by the smokehouse.

Then the whole flaming roof seemed to glitter redly up into the sky, and all the countryside

within a half mile was lit as if by the sun. Across
the hollow, up at the barbed-wire gap gate, Aaron
could make out a white sedan, a Ford Galaxie
maybe. And while he was trying to figure out who
it might belong to, the car's headlamps went to
high beams.

He looked down again at his father, who also
had become aware of the sedan. He was shading
his eyes with the hand not clutching the shotgun,
gazing up at the gap gate and paying no mind to
the figure who had just stolen around the far
corner of the smokehouse and was closing on his
back.

The white man had a club in his hand and was
already rearing it back to strike.

"Papa!" Aaron shouted.

But the roar of the fire must have been too loud
where Vertis was standing, for he continued to
stare up toward the car lights.

Aaron tried again, screaming this time: "Papa,
look behind now!"

But it was too late.

Vertis dropped to the dust, letting go of his
shotgun.

The white man picked it up, inspected the muzzle and the stock before flinging the piece into the
flames. A few seconds later, the two rounds cooked
off with a twin blast.

Aaron bit his fist.

He told his feet to carry him down the slope to
his father's prostrate body, but his feet wouldn't
move.

Now a second white man stepped up out of the
orange butterfly weed behind the smokehouse—
where he'd been hiding on his belly—and strolled
over to have a long look at Vertis. His mouth was

open like he was laughing. And he was hefting a coil of rope over his shoulder.

Aaron's mother made been making little gasping noises, but now seeing the rope she went quiet again, as unnaturally quiet as tonight's crickets and frogs, as quiet as snowfall.

With his heart racing so fast it almost hurt, he gazed down again in time to see his father's legs being dragged out of sight behind the level of the roofline of the house.

Then Aaron realized that he was sprinting back down the slope.

Yet when he had arrived in the yard between the house and the barn, his father and the white men were nowhere to be seen. Then he heard laughter on the road leading up to the gap gate. Creeping along the side of the smokehouse, showing no more than a sliver of his face around its corner, he caught sight of the ofays. They were striding toward their car, talking. "When that old nigger come out waving that scatter gun," one of them was saying, "he scairt the bejesus out of me."

But Vertis was not with them.

He raced to the far side of the yard, calling softly for his father. But then he sank to his knees.

His father was hanging limply from his mother's chinaberry tree, his toes within inches of touching the ground. The ofays had picked it not because it was the tallest tree on the farm, but the handiest.

Then Vertis gave a shudder and a kick.

"Papa!" Aaron yelped, running up to the base of the chinaberry. The rope was tied off low around the trunk, but the knot was too tight for him trembling fingers.

Then he remembered the ax embedded in the

chopping stump outside the kitchen door. "Hold on, Papa," he wept, "don't die, Papa!"

All the way to the stump and back again to the tree with the long-hafted ax in his hands, he despised himself for talking to the FBI men, for bringing this upon his father. He promised Jesus that if his father only lived, he would be more like his mother and say little if anything from now on, so help him God.

It took three blows to sever the rope.

Then his father plummeted heavily to the earth.

Still weeping, Aaron yanked again and again on the noose until some slack came into it. Then he slapped his father's cheek as hard as he could. And then once more.

Vertis made a retching sound, then started choking.

Aaron hugged him for a moment, then broke away and filled his hands with dust, which he flung skyward as if it were an offering.

There was a crash and a great shower of sparks as the barn tumbled in on itself.

Ward and Anderson stood on the concrete platform of the Jackson station until the last car in the departing train was a silver speck wavering in the mid-afternoon heat shimmers. Then it was gone, and the creosote and urine smells of the ties below seemed to well up and assault Ward's nostrils. He started walking past a baggage wagon on whose bed two aged Negro handlers were sprawled, awaiting the arrival of the next train. Anderson caught up with him a moment later, chewing pensively on a wad of spearmint. "Care to get ourselves an early supper before we drive back down to town?"

Ward had previously briefed him that the White

Citizens' Council was planning a rally at dusk in a field a mile outside town—as "a positive counterpoint to the colored violence" of two days before, a leaflet had declared. It remained to be seen if this gathering would be nonviolent, so they might not get another chance to eat. "Sure," Ward said after a moment, "it will be nice to eat something without wondering if the cook spit in it."

Anderson chuckled wearily. "Hell, I'd be happy if that's all he did to it."

Ward gave one more glance north—up the glinting rails that appeared to snake because of the haze mirages. "At least the Williams family is safe."

"Lucky they had kin in Chicago."

"Sometimes I wish every last one of them had kin up North. Or if not all of them, the bright and sensitive ones like Aaron."

"What good would that do?" Anderson asked, but not sounding particularly argumentative; both of them were too tired for that. "What if we could relocate every colored man, woman, and child up to Chicago, Detroit, and Newark? If the truth was told, things aren't any better for them up there. Maybe worse. At least down here they're not packed in tenements. And they know which white cops to give a wide berth."

"Perhaps you're right," Ward said quietly, passing a news kiosk and relieved to see that for once the headlines had nothing to do with the FBI in Mississippi. As surprising as it seemed, there were other things going on in the world. Lyndon Johnson was getting ready for his nominating convention in Atlantic City. If not for Dallas, Ward mused wistfully, this would be the kickoff for JFK's second term. Agents were not supposed to be so naive as to have political heroes, particularly ones at odds with the director, but he had wept that November day nine months before.

"Maybe that's what gets Dixie so pissed off. This is a national problem, not just a regional one." Anderson spat his gum into a wire trash basket. "Not saying there aren't differences in how North and South treat Negroes, mind you. There are. Like the old saying goes—down South, white folks don't care how close colored folks get, as long as they don't get uppity. Up North, they don't care how uppity the colored are, as long as they don't get close."

"I suppose." They emerged onto the sun-bright street. "Can you recommend some place good, Rupert?"

Only when Anderson looked at him strangely did Ward realize that it was the first time he'd ever called the man by his first name.

"You bet, Al," Anderson said after a moment, "nice little chicken joint around the corner here on Hanging Moss Road."

They walked in silence for a few blocks, their hands in their trouser pockets.

Then Ward blurted, "I'm not stupid, you know."

"Never said you were." Anderson seemed taken aback. "What brought that on?"

Ward laughed self-consciously. "That didn't come out the way I meant it." The truth was, he'd been dogged with such an overpowering sense of futility in the forty-eight hours since the attempt on Vertis Williams's life, he didn't know what he really meant. "I'm probably saying I'm not so dense that I don't realize"—his eyes had begun to smart, maddening him, but there was no turning back now—"that we're not making as much progress down here as we should be. And that we've gone somewhat astray from our original goal."

"To find the three VEP kids?"

Ward nodded, feeling no better now that he'd admitted his failing to Anderson.

"I'll go along with that," Anderson said—none too gently, which made it easier for Ward to then say:

"I'd like to ask you something personal."

"Shoot."

"Do you have special feelings for Mrs. Pell?"

"Hell yes," Anderson said, altogether too lightly, "who wouldn't for that pretty little lady?"

"I mean, have you fallen for her?

Anderson stopped walking. His face was grim, and he was glaring at Ward. "What in the name of God gives you the right to ask something like that?"

"My job."

Anderson's angry expression turned to one of the puzzlement. "What?"

"Because if you're in love with her, I'll understand and forgive your refusal to pursue the only chance we have of cracking this thing. If not, I'm going to have to start leaning on you. She's our only hope. Without her help, I'm going to fail down here, Rupert. And the thought of that is driving me nuts."

13

"I love Mississippi." Clayton Townley's amplified voice rolled out into the makeshift dirt parking lot, where Ward and a team of five other agents were jotting down license plate numbers—especially the out-of-state ones—and shining flashlights in the interiors of the cars and pickups for visible weapons. "They hate Mississippi," the grand wizard of the White Knights went on. "They hate us because we present a shining example of how segregation can work to the benefit of both white *and* colored."

Ward glanced up from an Alabama plate and then peered through the sparse foliage of a line of oaks at the torchlit platform from which Townley was holding court. The guttering torches suggested a Klan rally, although these were the only trappings of the "invisible empire" at the thousand-strong rally.

So far the agents had gone unnoticed, even though Ward was taking no special pains to keep his people out of sight. If trouble developed, so be it; he had had this attitude since returning from Jackson. He was no longer certain whether it was his good or bad anger that was pushing against the backs of his eyes, causing a dull, chronic pain.

"You know, folks, these northern students, dancing to the tune of their atheist communist bosses, who poured into our communities this summer to found their so-called 'freedom schools'—they have already failed in their secret mission to destroy our way of life. Their invasion has been repulsed by worthy men and women of the South who knew from the first white buds of spring that what we do together this summer will determine the fate of all Christian civilization for ages to come!"

Ward shook his head at the harsh, riotous clapping that followed these words. There was contempt even in the way these people applauded.

He had sent Anderson to relieve the agent who was presently posted inside Willie's house with a Thompson submachine gun and ten magazines of ammunition. The young witness and his widowed mother would be guarded around the clock until they could be relocated to relatives in Texas. The Bureau would handle the sale of their property, one more duty for him to discharge along with the thousands of others that had been hatched by this endless investigation. But Ward knew that he had virtually no hope of receiving any more Negro cooperation unless he could assure the security of those who had already stuck their necks out for him. And that involved dipping deeply in the federal witness-protection coffers in order to set these people up with new lives outside Mississippi. But Anderson's point at the train station this afternoon had been well taken: Ward couldn't evacuate every Negro out of the state; there were already grumblings from the Bureau's legal division about this bordering on constitutional abuse, even if the people were willingly allowing themselves to be moved.

"How do I know that these invaders have failed?" Townley's voice boomed, followed by a squeal of feedback. "Because, my friends, of all the federal policemen I see about me—prying, prying into our private lives, searching our God-given property, violating our civil liberties with impunity. But they too are powerless against the justness of our cause, powerless because every last Anglo-Saxon Christian one of us stands together!" His torchlit eyes glinted as he paused. "Will we continue to stand shoulder to shoulder?"

"Yes!" came the ferociously defiant response, which left Ward with a prickling sensation on the back of his neck, as if he'd just heard an echo of a Nuremberg rally.

"Will we become a spear on which the atheist enemy impales himself?"

"Yes!"

"This week, my brothers and sisters, in the courts of the great state of Mississippi, they have been reminded that they cannot forcibly make our communities into little replicas of their own chaos—in which Negroes run riot, unrestrained and unpunished, as they do this very summer in the streets of Harlem, and in the street of Oakland, and in the streets of Chicago!"

The slap on the wrist the defendants had received for burning out Obie Walker had emboldened the local peckerwoods: Ward and his agents were now receiving threats, some amounting to anonymous whispers over the phone, but others issued with far less timidity. Frankly, he wasn't sure what to do about it. He didn't want to be suckered into losing his temper, particularly with media following him nearly everywhere he went in the county, but neither did he want to let these challenges go unpunished.

"Mr. Ward?" John Byrd called from the line of oaks, where he'd been keeping watch on the proceedings through binoculars. "Men on the way."

Ward noticed the cluster of torches bobbing toward the parking lot. "Everybody stand easy," he said to his agents.

In the vanguard of the group of six men was Clinton Pell, in civilian dress. The pitchy flames of the torch he was holding made his face seemed flat and obstinate. He walked directly up to Ward and revealed that he was armed by parting his jacket as he placed his right hand on his hip.

On the edge of his vision, Ward was reassured to see one of his agents casually lean over the hood of a pickup. The best handgun marksman in the group, he was furtively giving himself a bench-rest shot at Pell in case the deputy lost his head and drew on Ward. He found himself wishing that Pell might do this.

"You got no goddamn right snooping around here, Hoover boy. This here is political meeting guaranteed by the First Amend—"

"Any of you Lester Cowens?" Ward asked, grinning even though he was suddenly angrier than he'd thought possible on such short notice. Perhaps Pell's snarl had done it to him, or hearing 'Hoover boy' for the hundredth time this week. Or perhaps it was the unexpected certainty that what he was now feeling was his good anger, the same molten stuff that had made him quit his fraternity and endure the social Siberia that followed.

"I'm Cowens." The biggest man in the group

stepped forward; he was even more massive than Frank Bailey. "Why?"

"I heard you want to tear off my head so you can shit down my windpipe."

Cowens smirked. "Could be."

All at once, Ward was working not to control his anger, but to keep it hot, for he knew that if it faded he would be frightened to death: the man had seventy pounds on him, and most of those looked to be farm labor muscle. He reminded himself that here stood the man who had clubbed Vertis Williams and then kicked young Aaron in the ribs. "Could be or not, Cowens? Make up your mind."

"What crawled up your ass, boy?"

"You, Cowens, with your loud mouth. And I'm here to kick your ass."

Cowens stopped smirking.

Behind him Ward could sense his agents shifting around uneasily.

"What about your gun?" Cowens asked. "I got no gun on me."

"Mr. Byrd?" He handed over his revolver to the agent. "Please hang on to this for me."

"No way, hoss." Cowens was slowly shaking his head. "The minute you start losing, one of your ladies here is gonna drill me right between the eyes. Then y'all swear up and down in court I attacked you. Every last one of you will swear it on a stack of Bibles."

"Gentlemen," Ward announced over his shoulder to his agents, "under no circumstances are you to resort to gunplay in my behalf. In the unlikely event I lose, you are to keep your weapons holstered. Do you understand me?"

The agents mumbled or nodded that they did.

"And I emphasize 'unlikely event,'" Ward said between clenched teeth, his voice shaking from what was now a richly satisfying rage, "because I'm going to clean this bastard's clock for him!" He raised his fists and stepped forward.

"Bullshit!" Cowens said, withdrawing into the midst of his friends. "That boy's touched. Do something, Clinton!"

"This is gonna be reported to your bosses," Pell said triumphantly. "You're history around here, Hoover boy. Assault is a misdemeanor in this state, and I got a dozen witnesses to it!"

Ward hesitated, then slowly lowered his fists. "I'll save you the trouble of reporting it, shit-for-brains." Turning for his Dodge, he said to his agents, "Let's go."

As soon as they arrived back at the theater, Ward separated himself from the others and began pacing the mezzanine, trying to think of some way out of the predicament he had just created for himself. But after only a few minutes, he stopped walking and declared under his breath, "Son of a bitch, I've still got my honesty. I can take that much away from this goddamned job."

Then he made for the telephone downstairs.

He reached the inspector at home on the second ring: "Ward here, sir."

"How's it going down there, Alan?"

"Sir, something happened tonight for which I believe I should be relieved."

The inspector paused, then said, "Please explain yourself."

"We're running up against something new. Something rather unexpected. They're trying to physically intimidate us now."

"How serious is it?"

"If allowed to continue, it will be extremely serious. I believe that it will eventually invite violence against us and even worse violence against those we're trying to protect."

"So what have you been doing about it?"

Ward took a quick, sharp breath. "That's the problem I wanted to discuss, sir. A local threatened me personally this afternoon. I confronted him this evening. I challenged him to a fight. This was in front of witnesses."

Silence followed on the other end of the line.

"I apologize for my behavior, sir—and will understand if I'm pulled out of here. There is no excuse for what I did."

"Where are you now?"

"Our theater command post."

"Please stay there, Alan. I'll get back to you shortly."

"All right, sir."

Ward hung up. A shadow passed over him. It was John Byrd, offering him a bottle of Coca-Cola. "Thanks."

"You're welcome, Mr. Ward."

He took a swallow, avoiding Byrd's inquisitive gaze. "I'd like to apologize to you and other guys. Something just snapped, I guess."

"No apologies necessary."

Ward nodded, then fell silent, his eyes glazing over as they settled on the telephone. "I'm so damned sick of their faces, John, their hostile and ignorant fucking faces."

Ten minutes later, the phone rang.

Instead of the inspector it was Director Hoover himself, calling—as he explained—from the president's Oval Office, where he was making his nightly report on the Mississippi situation. "I've just been told some of the boys down there don't think the law applies to them."

"That's correct, sir."

"Well, nobody is going to make a threat against one of my men. Is that what happened, Ward?"

"Yes, sir."

"Then here's the word—a face-to-face showdown with any hardcase who tries to bulldoze us is all right with me. Mind you, I'm talking about keeping it to a little bare-knuckle stuff, and it ought to be in self-defense. But I'm leaving it up to your people to figure out what constitutes self-defense. Do we have an understanding?"

"Very good, sir." In the background, Ward could hear the president saying, "Tell that boy to keep up the steam, Edgar. Tell him, full-court press."

"Did you hear the president?" the director asked.

"I did, sir."

"Same goes for me. Full-court press. Anything else to report?"

"No, sir . . . I'm afraid not."

"Good night, Ward."

He replaced the receiver in the cradle, overlapping his hands behind his head, and let out a long breath.

At ten o'clock Anderson was relieved of guard duty at young Willie's house, where, in the absence of anything else to do, he'd helped the boy and his mother prepare supper. He drove south along the state highway through a night rife with bugs, all the way to Louisiana border thirty miles distant before turning around and cruising back to town.

The lights were on inside the beauty parlor.

He backed up so he could look through the glass front door.

Surprisingly, she was still there, mopping up.

He parked on the next side street and strolled back to the shop, trying to think of something both clever and decent to say. The door was unlocked, and he stepped inside, clearing his throat.

The neon ceiling fixtures were buzzing with an illumination that was vaguely bluish, like skim milk.

Her gaze darted up from the wet linoleum and fastened on him. He believed that her grip tightened around the handle of the mop.

"You shouldn't be here," she said.

"I know."

"I mean it."

"I saw the lights on." His voice sounded to him as if it were coming from someplace outside his head. "Nobody saw me."

She repeated the flat truth that he shouldn't be here, and he nodded in a way he hoped would be taken for an apology. He glanced at the glistening floor. "You're working late."

Suddenly, holding the mop seemed to embarrass her, and he was sorry he'd drawn her attention to it.

"The colored lady who ordinarily does this hasn't shown up since the trial," she said, leaning the mop against one of the chairs.

Again he nodded. She crossed her arms over her bust.

"Are we such awful people down here, Mr. Anderson?"

He didn't know what to say. Although he ached to reassure her, everything he thought of drowned in a wash of ridiculousness before he could come out with it. He came close to walking out without shaming himself with another word.

"I mean," she went on, rubbing the backs of her bare arms as if she were cold, "we were taught from being little babies that segregation is what God planned for us, weren't we, now? And that the colored were born to a lower life, serving us? Weren't we, now?"

"Genesis nine, verses twenty-six and seven," he said, hating to see her face twisted by the agony that had taken hold of her since he'd last seen her. He sensed that if it went on long enough, this misery would make her waste away; she did not know how to take things lightly. "Blessed by the Lord my God be Shem; and let Canaan be his slave. God enlarge Japheth, and let him dwell in the tents of Shem; and let Canaan be his slave."

"Yes!" she said, hysterically almost. He took a step toward her, but she withdrew two steps. "I wanted to phone her, you know."

"Who?"

"Our colored woman. I wanted to tell her that I don't think what happened at the courthouse this week was right. To tell her that, yes, I was born to the hate, I lived it all my life, even married it—but it doesn't own me. The hate doesn't own me, Mr. Anderson—like it does some."

"Then why didn't you phone her?"

"Naomi doesn't have one," she said. "And I'm scared to go down to her house. You'd go down there if you were me, wouldn't you, Mr. Anderson?" She had begun to cry, but then fended him off with a flat-handed gesture when he tried once more to approach her. "Tell the truth, now."

"I'm not so sure I know what I'd do."

"Then are you as messed up about this as I am?" she asked hopefully.

"More so, sweet lady. And they even trusted me with a gun to try to sort it all out."

Just when he expected her to smile, she began watching him with eyes that had grown small and lightless with suspicion. "Why'd you come to see me tonight, Mr. Anderson?"

He hesitated before saying, "The boss man sent me to find out about those fifty minutes your husband supposedly spent with you that night." The sudden anger in her face made him feel sick to his stomach.

"And if I don't tell you?"

"It won't change anything."

"You mean the truth won't help change anything around here?" She looked as if she'd been slapped.

Then, turning, she hurried for the back room, sidling through the part in the floor-length curtains.

After staring at the curtains until they hung still again, he started out the front door, but stopped. Then he rushed for the back room before he could change his mind again.

She was leaning against the far wall in the dimness.

"I didn't come here for the fifty minutes. I coulda settled that one way or another a long time ago. I came because I needed to see you again."

She dried her cheeks with the back of her hand. "My daddy warned me never to burn my bridges. I had no idea what he meant until now. Maybe I believed I didn't have any bridges worth saving. Do I, Mr. Anderson?"

She didn't resist when he closed his arms around her and drew her into him. "Be quiet . . . please."

"My husband drove one of the cars that night."
He shut his eyes. "Oh, Christ."

"It's what you want to hear, isn't it?"

"No . . . no."

"The bodies are buried on the Roberts' farm. In
the new earthen dam." A sob convulsed her shoulders, and he held her tighter. "What are you going
to do now?" she asked.

He kissed her.

The Roberts' farm was several miles east of the
black earth of the Delta country, so the dirt embankment of the dam was blood red. Ward watched
the bucket of the backhoe cut into it, then withdraw as the operator retracted the boom. Each
time he expected to see something, and each time
he was relieved that nothing had come into view.

The V-shaped slash was now within ten feet of
completely breaching the dam the agents had finished draining at dawn. The pile of mud depos-
ited in the pasture by the backhoe was steaming
under the noon sun.

Shoes scuffled the ground behind Ward, and he
turned to see Anderson, who was returning once
again from checking the agents posted along the
perimeter. He had charged him with providing
security to the site, believing that the discovery of
the bodies might at long last trigger an armed
response from the suspects—and that Anderson,
with his combat infantry experience, would know
best how to counter such an attack.

"How's it look?" Ward asked.

Anderson was gazing down into the muddy slash.
"Quiet. But I told the boys to keep using their
cover. If they try to hit us today, it'll be a sniper
play—I'd bet on it."

John Byrd was poised at the brink of the slash, his hands braced on his knees.

"See anything, John?" Anderson called out to him.

"Nothing yet."

Then Anderson muttered so only Ward could hear, "Well, you'll smell anything before you see it."

"What kind of shape do you think they'll be in?" Ward asked tentatively. "For identification purposes, I mean."

"After damn near a month in warm, wet ground?" Anderson didn't answer his own question. Instead he said, "I think we should start easing up with the backhoe and get a man down there with a shovel every five bucketfuls or so."

"You volunteering, Rupert?"

"Not this old dogface. I'm allergic to mud."

"Nice thing about that Belgian cold," Anderson said absently, "was there there was absolutely no putrefaction. But, then again, our poor wounded bastards were freezing where they lay. Freezing to death in the blink of an eye. A bleeding man just can't take low temperatures."

"Are you ready to be spelled, Mr. Byrd?" Ward shouted down into the backhoe slash. The sweaty, coverall-clad agent was now lifting each shovelful of red clay as if it weighed a hundred pounds. "You look like you can use a rest."

"Another ten minutes, sir. I think it's more work to crawl out of this pit. Give me another—" Byrd was peering at a slab of mud that had just crumbled off the embankment.

"What is it?" Ward asked.

"I think you better have a look, sir," Byrd said with a strange new timbre to his voice.

Ward and Anderson quickly slid down on their heels, muddying their fingers as they clawed to a stop beside Byrd. In those seconds the agent had gone sickly pale.

Ward found that he couldn't take his eyes off the rotting hand. It was jutting out of the clay, cricked in such a way that it seemed to be beseeching help. "Is it our Negro victim?"

"No way of telling," Anderson said. "White and black together wind up that purply color, especially if they lay out in the sun a full day before being covered up. Mr. Byrd?"

"Sir?" On the verge of heaving, he was swallowing down his saliva fast and furious.

"I'd like you to go up and get the canteen under the front seat of Mr. Ward's car. Moisten your handkerchief and tie it around your nose and mouth. Then tote on down the water for Mr. Ward. Oh—there's some old stogies in the glove box. They're half tobacco and half Goodyear rubber. I'd be much obliged if you brought one down for me." Then he added, a bit shamefaced: "Only occasion I smoke anymore."

As Byrd scrambled wordlessly up the slope, Ward said, "We'll all have a turn at the digging from now on."

"Won't work, Al." Anderson reached for the shovel. "Some boys can't deal with it. Not that they're cowards or anything. But they just don't have the stomach for it." He gently sank the blade of the shovel into the soggy dirt below the hand. As he removed the shovelful and tossed it aside, the decomposed hand nearly separated from the wrist. Apologetically almost, he looked at Ward. "How you doing?"

Ward nodded that he was all right.

"Good, I figured as much. If that didn't turn your guts, the rest won't. How about hunting up another shovel?"

The county coroner was the local mortician, and it was into the embalming room of his mortuary the three bodies were carried by Ward's agents. During the ten minutes he and Anderson were inside, warning the coroner not to touch the decedents until the Bureau's lab man and a pathologist could arrive from Jackson, a horde of newsmen ringed the building.

"Mr. Ward," one of them shouted above the tumult when Anderson and he emerged into the glare of television lights, "how did you come by the information that led to the grave site?"

Ward could feel Anderson go tense beside him. "Dogs, gentlemen."

"What was that, Mr. Ward?"

"We've been using special bloodhounds for the past few weeks. Searching acre by acre. It finally paid off."

Anderson seemed to relax, but not much.

14

Sitting at his desk in the sheriff's office, Clinton Pell reached for his telephone for the fifth time in the past hour. Two calls had been from nervous Nellies who thought they'd seen niggers skulking around their backyards. He wasn't even responding to those anymore; two had been from weak sisters, a couple of the boys hemming and hawing for a stroke of reassurance that the FBI finding the bodies today didn't mean jackshit. And now this one, a damned whisperer.

"Speak up," Pell said while lighting up a Pall Mall. "I can't hear you. What—?"

The match never touched his cigarette. It had tumbled from his fingers and was smoldering out on the blotter.

He told the caller to repeat herself, which she did, apparently with a hankie or a rag over the phone. Then he asked, "And when was this?"

Last night, she informed him.

"And you swear to this?"

She told him that she was willing to die with the statement in her mouth.

"Then tell who you are, woman."

But she had hung up.

*   *   *

Rain was on the way.

Through her kitchen window Mrs. Pell watched pale flarings along the horizon—distant lightning. She sipped her evening crème de menthe and tried to decide if he would settle for bologna and Swiss cheese tonight. But her thoughts kept returning to thoughts about the rain. It would be good, a hard fall. It would cool things off, maybe even cool people off, leave them mellow and satisfied just to hear the dripping noises off the eaves.

Then she started.

The screen door had been slammed so forcefully she was sure it'd been torn off the hinges.

He was running through the living room. But he halted at the kitchen door and just stood there for a long moment. His patrolman's cap was cocked back from his sweaty forehead. There was no sound except his hard wheezing.

Her eyes swept from her husband's face to the rear door, but she had no real hope of escape.

"Hello, Clinton," she said at last, wearily.

The first blow was to her ear, and she felt blood trickle down the lobe and over her neck.

Yet she was still standing afterward. This was somewhat of a disappointment, for she had wanted to be knocked unconscious right away. She hadn't even minded the thought of him kicking her as she lay on the floor—as he had done once before— for she'd come to that time with bruises all over her face and a loose tooth.

His second punch flung her across the kitchen table, and her falling weight broke it in two. She tumbled through the leaves and landed hard on her elbows against the floor.

Her eyes were now on the same level as his black boots.

Immediately he seized her and sat her upright so he could slap her. He used both the palm and back of his hand repeatedly.

Then he stopped slapping to grab her roughly by the ears.

Her vision grew bleary, then found a focus again. It was funny, but in the midst of this she could not despise Clinton Pell, who was driving her face against his uplifted knee again and again.

Anderson had been asleep only a half hour when the phone rang on the nightstand. Fumbling for the receiver, he dunked his fingers in his half-finished glass of bourbon. "Yeah . . . Anderson here."

It was John Byrd. "Sorry to wake you, sir."

"That's okay." He squinted as the phosphorescent dial of his wristwatch: ten after two. "I had to get up to answer the goddamn phone anyways."

"Mr. Ward wants you to get over to the hospital ASAP."

"What's happened?" He sat up and rubbed his sleep-numbed face with his hand. "One of our people get hurt?"

"I'm sorry, Mr. Anderson, I'm not to say anything more over the landline."

"Understood, on my way."

Flicking on the lamp, he blinked around the room for his trousers, located them on the back of a chair. His change jingled in his pockets as he wrestled into his pants.

One of the agents had been shot. It was as clear as day to him. In an environment with as many privately owned guns and as many ragged tempers as Mississippi had, it'd only been a matter of time.

Ward had been shot once before himself, but Anderson doubted that he'd ever handled an agent-involved shooting. There was one helluva lot to do investigatively and administratively, not to mention getting a man from the field office in the wounded or dead agent's hometown to tell his little woman that what she'd always feared had finally happened. Anderson himself had been ordered to deliver such news twice; he counted both occasions among the worst of his life.

"Damn this job," he said, buttoning yesterday's shirt—no use wrinkling a fresh one before morning.

"Damn," he repeated, stepping out the door and realizing that there wasn't a Dodge Polara on the lot. The entire motor pool had been checked out. And it was raining.

The hospital was no more than a quarter mile from the motel, so he snugged his jacket collar to keep the rain from running down his neck and started trotting.

Within a hundred yards his feet began bothering him, and he expected a sideache any moment.

There was lightning in the southwest, but far away he had yet to hear thunder.

Shortness of breath forced him to walk the last block to the hospital.

Two agents were posted out front, holding umbrellas. Now he was convinced that it had been fatal. Jesus, had Ward himself been gunned down and had Byrd only being playing it coy until he could confer with the senior-most agent, none other than Rupert Anderson?"

"Who bought it?" he asked, but neither of the

agents answered him. And they were sneaky-eyed to boot, which he found unsettling.

Byrd met him inside. "You're soaked."

"No shit. Now tell me what the hell's going on."

"She's critical, but that might well be down-graded in the morning."

Anderson stopped walking. He knew at once who Byrd was talking about. His dazed mind made the shift from a wounded agent to her, but clung to the notion of gunplay. "Was she shot?" he asked.

"No, beaten. Badly, Mr. Anderson. A neighbor heard the commotion and found her unconscious in the kitchen. But nobody's really talking, as usual. Although we're pretty sure it was her husband."

"Which room is she?" He was already moving again.

"Turn right next corridor. You'll see Brodsky manning the door."

Anderson started running, ignoring a night or-derly's admonition. Sweeping past Brodsky with-out a greeting, he shut the door behind him and shuffled into the center of the darkened room, where he stood waiting for his eyes to adjust to lackluster glow of the night-light. The rainwater running off his clothes was pattering against the floor.

"Over here, Rupert," Ward said softly from the chair in the corner.

Anderson ignored him and approached the bed. By now he could make out her face. It was horri-bly bruised; a tube was snaking up her nose.

"She's going to be okay, Rupert."

He continued to stare at her silently.

"I talked to the doctor not ten minutes ago," Ward went on with the unmistakable edge of guilt to his voice. "She's going to be taken off the critical list soon. They were worried about internal bleeding, but apparently that's not a problem. Still, she's not doing much talking. But she's going to pull through."

Anderson began to silently cry, his big shoulders trembling as he clasped himself. He really couldn't do it here, not with Ward in the same room with him. So instead of crying he made up his mind to kill Clinton Pell. In the white-hot clarity of the instant the notion offered perfect and absolute sense. Pell was going to die tonight, die screaming for mercy.

He wanted to touch her hand before he left the room. But it lay buried under the covers, so he just stroked the blanket where he thought her forearm might be.

Then he strode out the door.

Ward had followed him. "Rupert, wait."

Anderson kept walking toward the red exit sign at the far end of the corridor.

"Stop." Ward made a grab for his sleeve, but Anderson shook off his hand.

"Go to hell, Boss."

"I'm telling you to stop. And I mean it." The young agent leaned on his arm against the door as Anderson reached for the bar latch. Ward studied his face, and what he saw there apparently made him say, "We're not killers, Rupert. That's the difference between them and us."

"That's the difference between them and you."

"No, no—"

"I know what I am, and I accept it." Anderson jerked the latch, but Ward continued to press his weight against the door.

The two agents on sentry duty outside were gaping through the rain-speckled glass, looking confused. "Everything okay, Mr. Ward?" one of them worked up the nerve to ask.

Ward nodded with a frown, then turned back to Anderson. "You're not any more like them than I am."

"What do you care what I do to one son of a bitch hiding behind a sheriff's star? Don't you have the whole world to change?" Then Anderson hurled open the door, driving Ward ten feet back into the corridor.

The cool rain felt good: it reminded to turn his anger cold. He would need a cold anger if he intended to get Clinton Pell tonight. The bastard was most likely expecting him to react and would be lying in wait.

"That's right," Ward said from behind, having caught up with him again. "And I'm changing it, Rupert. You're changing it, too. Haven't you noticed? Since we uncovered the bodies, the pricks aren't laughing anymore. They know now we're here to stay—and playing for keeps."

Anderson paused at the sidewalk. He had just realized that he had no car. "Give me your keys."

"No."

He seized Ward by the shirt front. "Give me the damn keys, Ward."

"What're you going to do? Shake me upside down?"

"I just might."

"No, you're not. And unless you let go of me right this second I'm going to shoot you, Rupert."

Anderson came close to laughing.

But then, with an inscrutable look coming into his eyes, Ward drew his revolver and rested the muzzle against Anderson's Adam's apple. "If you go after Pell like this you're going to have to do it right through the middle of me. I hate what he did to her almost as much as you do. But damn you, Anderson, I'm not going to watch this entire investigation crash and burn because of your personal feelings about a witness."

"Don't confuse drawing a gun and using it, Boss. A man oughta know himself down to the marrow before he ever draws on another man. A man oughta accept what he is."

Ward chuckled as he thumbed back the hammer. For the first time Anderson felt a flicker of alarm.

"Oh, I'm accepting all kinds of things about myself, Rupert. Like I got a temper, one just as quick and nasty as yours. Except mine has a much shorter fuse. Did you hear I challenged Lester Cowens to a fistfight?"

"No."

Ward's eyelids were twitching from the raindrops. "Well, I did."

"In front of witnesses?"

"A baker's dozen of them."

"That'll get back to Washington."

"It already has," Ward said, chuckling again in that disquieting way.

Anderson suspected that it was an act, but presently didn't feel like testing the man's sincerity, not with a cocked revolver jammed in his throat.

"I told the inspector exactly what happened and asked to be relieved," Ward went on. "He relayed my little indiscretion to the director, who phoned me from the White House. Both Johnson and he informed me that it's a new game—full-court press, they said. Bare-knuckle stuff in self-defense has been sanctioned. And they left it up to us to decide what constitutes self-defense." He grinned.

"Would you listen to me, you big, dumb peckerwood? We've just been handed a license to do it your way!"

At last Anderson unhanded him. Nudging Ward's revolver aside, he wiped the rainwater off the tip of his nose. "Holster that piece before you got something to explain to Mr. Hoover."

"They want me to say, 'Let us not forget that two white boys also died helping us Negroes help ourselves.'" The preacher paused to stroke one of his salt-and-pepper muttonchops whiskers as if he were in the midst of a great perplexity. "They want me to say, 'We mourn with the mothers of these two white boys.'"

A member of the congregation gave out with an amen which proved premature, for the preacher then said:

"But how, brother and sisters, can we properly mourn those two white boys when the grand and glorious state of Mississippi won't even allow those white boys to be buried in the same cemetery as this Negro boy?!"

Now came a chorus of amens. Ward shifted a bit uneasily in his pew. The resentment surrounding him was beginning to feel as oppressive as the humidity. He did not want another riot, not at the auspicious moment in which the wall of silence around the murders was beginning to crumble: a *white* caller, although remaining anonymous, had nevertheless informed the Bureau that Mayor Lyle Tilman "knows where to dot the i's and cross the t's." No doubt the caller had been someone with an old score to settle—what politician didn't have enemies? Yet the last thing Ward wanted was for

Negro unrest to suddenly force the white community to close ranks again.

". . . I say I have no more love to give, brothers and sisters." The preacher's voice welled back into Ward's attention. "I have only anger in my heart today, and I ask you to be angry along with me! I am sick and tired, and I ask you to be sick and tired along with me! I am sick and tired of officiating at the funerals of black men who have been cut down by white men!"

The roar was so deafening Ward didn't hear John Byrd sidle in beside him. The agent had been manning the telephone in the church office: their only means of communication with the command post in the theater, for they had driven sixty miles and across three Mississippi counties to attend this service and to make sure that the state troopers were providing adequate security. "Mr. Anderson," Byrd whispered in his ear, "informs me that he's ready."

"Is he still on the line?"

Byrd nodded.

"Tell him to take along some iodine in case his knuckles get skinned."

Byrd smiled meaningfully, then returned to the office.

"Brother and sisters, I also ask you to be sick and tired of those people in this country who with their silence and indifference and advice for us to be patient continue and continue to allow these things to happen. What is an 'inalienable' right if your skin is black? What does it truly mean—'equal treatment under the law?' What does it mean now—'liberty and justice for all?!' "

Ward was no longer sure. But one thing he did know: it would be sweet to get in some licks of his own against those who had been obstructing even the barest definition of American justice for more than a month.

Anderson and Brodsky were almost to the old Army Air Corps field that had lain abandoned on the edge of the county since the closing days of World War II when the pug-faced agent asked, "You see that, Mr. Anderson?"

"No, what?" Driving the Dodge Polara, he had been deep in his own thoughts. Nevertheless, it was a bad sign that he was still half blind with rage. He would never forgive himself if his inattention got a brother agent hurt.

"One of the crackers drinking around the pickup parked back in the woods there, he brandished a shotgun at us."

"Like he was going to open fire?"

"More like he was just horsing around. But who's to say?"

"Well," Anderson said, locking the brakes and spinning the sedan around in a pall of its own tire smoke, "I think this boy should be taught that there's no horsing around where firearms is involved."

"Amen," Brodsky said.

"Hell, Alex, I didn't realize you were religious."

"Neither did I until I saw that goddamn shotgun being waved my way."

By the time they got back to the pickup, the offending gun was nowhere to be seen, and the four locals were grinning as if they'd pulled a good one on the agents.

Brodsky got out cautiously, keeping his right hand on his revolver and his eyes fastened on the men. Two were sitting on the tailgate, the other two leaning against the rear-wheel cowlings. All were drinking from fruit jars.

Anderson emerged from the Dodge with a shotgun in hand. "Afternoon, boys." Calmly clacking a round into the chamber, he then blew out the pickup's windshield, shredding the jack oaks beyond with the flying shards of glass. The front tire facing him was deflated with a second blast that echoed over the heads of the crackers, who were now prone in the dust.

"I think I got two on the wing, Alex," Anderson said. "Ain't it just dandy, this early bobwhite season?"

Brodsky shaded his eyes against the hot, blank sky as if scanning for gamebirds, then drew and with three .38-special rounds shattered two of the fruit jars on the tailgate.

"What'd you get, Alex?"

"A spruce grouse, I think."

"Sorry, no grouse in these parts."

"My mistake, then," Brodsky said contritely.

"Be more careful in the future. A fella should know exactly what he's aiming at before he pulls the trigger. That's what my daddy always told me."

"I'll remember from now on."

"See y'all next hunting season," Anderson said amicably to the men as Brodsky and he got back inside the sedan.

Through the years, weeds had poked up through the runway, but the pilot found enough clear asphalt to set his Cessna down. Anderson sped out to the plane just as a large Negro in a well-tailored business suit climbed down from the cockpit. The pilot handed him his suitcase, waited for him to walk well clear of the propeller, then revved the engine, and took off again.

Anderson got out and gave the Negro a quick hug before picking up his suitcase for him and stowing it in the trunk.

"Mr. Brodsky," he said as he began driving back across the disintegrating runway, "I'd like you to meet Mr. Monk."

They shook hands, but neither man said anything. Anderson enjoyed Brodsky's initial apprehension. Monk, with his hulking frame and habitual scowl, could be disquieting to behold.

"Are you new with the Bureau?" Brodsky finally asked.

The man just laughed as he watched the shadowy Mississippi woods slip past. It was a big, rumbling laugh without much humor in it.

Monk preferred not to advertise that he was a homicide detective with Chicago PD. Anderson had borrowed his services on several occasions before: a common enough arrangement the Bureau had established with a number of law-enforcement agencies around the country. Detective Gordon Monk was famous throughout the Midwest police community for the effect his stark countenance and looming presence had on the interrogation process. He had solicited a number of crucial confessions simply by staring at the suspect until he cracked; his technique was especially productive on Southerners who'd been transplanted to Chicago. Recalling this had given Anderson an idea.

"What's the deal, Roop?" Monk asked, yawning.

"Mayor down here knows enough to consider him dirty in the murder of our three kids."

"This old boy dirty otherwise?"

Anderson smiled: Monk had ready glimpsed the lure he was using to lure Lyle Tilman out into the countryside for a little chat with a large and intimidating Negro. "You bet, dirty as a Chi-town ward boss. This morning, one of our people posing as a Yankee businessman made an anonymous ring to his office, asking for a meeting outside town so as not to get the rumor mill churning. Now that you ask, our man did mention something about payola."

Monk laughed again, but this time with a bit more mirth. "I take this statement ain't intended to stand up in court."

"No, it's just to put us in the know so we can pull an end run later with the help of some of the other participants."

"Good, I hate going into these things with my hands tied behind my back. How long you gonna need me?"

"Just this evening, Mr. Monk. If all goes well, you'll be back at the airfield before midnight."

From the woods Anderson watched the headlamps of Lyle Tilman's Cadillac inch up the dirt road, the thick foliage scattering their light. They winked out in front of the unlit cabin, but it was at least a minute before the portly man's silhouette could be seen lumbering up the steps to the front door.

Tilman knocked and called out a soft hello.

"Enter," Monk said, congenially almost.

As Tilman crept inside the dark cabin, Brodsky whispered to Anderson, "What the hell is this guy Monk? Really?"

"Well, back in the Old West he woulda been

called a 'regulator.' You know, a hired gun brought in to beat the riffraff back under the rocks."

"Is he any good?"

At that moment a sound like clawing came from inside the front door of the cabin. It was followed by the unmistakable crash of a man being hurled against wooden furniture.

"He does all right," Anderson said.

Sprawling atop his motel bed, Anderson took a sip of bourbon, then went on: "Poor Brodsky, he thinks I brought in some colored Billy the Kid, a born killer."

"And what's the real Gordon Monk like?" Ward asked, pouring more sour mash into his his motel glass of Coca-Cola. He was beginning to appreciate bourbon—these few drinking sessions with Anderson were the only times he could recall relaxing in the past month.

"Oh hell, he's a regular pussycat. Don't drink and don't smoke. And his Baptist mama got her hooks in him so bad he don't even swear. That's why everybody in the homicide bull pen calls him 'Golly.' I can't blame old Tilman for spilling the beans the way he did. There's something terrifying about a colored man who don't swear."

Ward had decided to let Anderson unfold the results of the interrogation in his own way and at his own speed. Quite simply, he was satisfied that the man had not lapsed again into the lunatic single-mindedness he'd exhibited the night before, although he blamed himself for underestimating Anderson's feelings for Mrs. Pell. He promised himself that, whatever priorities he set for himself in the coming days, the foremost would be to be present when the inevitable showdown between

Clinton Pell and Rupert Anderson occurred. "Bare-knuckle stuff" did not include homicide.

"You sure Tilman won't talk about this?" Ward asked, trying not to sound uneasy at how the mayor had been treated tonight.

"Not a chance. First of all, he has no idea who did it to him. He was scampering toward an unexpected pot of gold when fate set a surly-looking Negro in his path. Second, he knows damn well the Klan would kill him. Can you imagine him telling Grand Wizard Clayton Townley that 'a big nigger I never seen before particularized the whole story out of me.' " Anderson chuckled to himself.

Ward saw by the level in the bottle that Anderson had drunk more than usual tonight, and sensed that he was worrying about her. "She said a few words to the nurse this evening," Ward volunteered.

Anderson's eyes clicked toward him.

"She asked about you, Rupert."

Anderson nodded, but not as if he were pleased. "Then her mind's okay, I suppose."

"Fine."

"She has a good mind, you know. She thinks about things you wouldn't expect her to. I mean, things most women in her situation don't bother with." Anderson gave his sad smile. "Damn if what she doesn't look at things the way you do, sorta."

"How's that?"

"Ah, you know, about this changing that and things being better for everybody some dandy day."

"Things will be, Rupert, if we hang in there."

"Whatever." Anderson stretched. "Well, let's go through Lyle Tilman's lyrics while they're still fresh in my mind."

"Care if I take notes?"

Anderson shrugged indifferently, and Ward

plucked his spiral pad from his coat, which he'd draped over the foot of the spare bed. The notes would be for the benefit of the inspector and ultimately the director. The former would have to be phoned as soon as this discussion was concluded. How would he say that this information had been developed? He had no intention of lying. Anderson's account distracted him from the dilemma.

"Three cars and seven men rode that night. Pell and Frank Bailey did the killing."

"You were right about Pell," Ward noted.

"Yeah, but in some ways I'd be glad to have been wrong." Anderson's eyes clouded briefly, but then turned incisive again. "High Sheriff Raymond Stuckey was in on it from the get-go. But just the logistics and the planning. He was too smart to be there with a gun smoking in his fist. Whatever we think of Stuckey, he's a cop. And there ain't a cop alive who'll put his trust in conspiracies of silence. Hell, that's how a cop earns his daily bread: cajoling or bribing or threatening folks into breaking their sacred vows of silence and ratting on their blood brothers. No, Stuckey sat this one out and we'll probably have a bitch of a time connecting him to it."

"How about Clayton Townley?" Ward asked, taking a slug of bourbon straight from the pint.

"It was all his brainchild. But if we find Stuckey did a thorough job of brushing out his tracks, it's nothing compared to how the head pointy-head covered his ass."

"Next point—how do we get something that will stand on its own legs in court?"

"A Mississippi court?" Anderson harrumphed. "Like my daddy used to declare—might as well try to break wind and paint it purple."

"I was thinking of federal court."

"Then I say we should quit dicking around in the hope of getting any murder convictions and concentrate on the Title Eighteen offenses. Besides, that gives us some maneuvering space with these hayseeds."

"How's that?" Ward asked.

"Well, we can track mud all over the homicide evidence as long we're clean as little white angels while investigating the civil-rights violations."

"When you say 'track mud,' do you mean duress and coercion?"

Anderson's face turned grim. "That's right, Al. It's more than what he gave her. He skipped the coercion and went straight to the duress. I just hope to return the favor before they start shitting on each other better than we could ever hope to."

15

The Grand Wizard of the White Knights of the Ku Klux Klan, Clayton Townley, struck the small Confederate battle flags from the front fenders of his new Oldsmobile convertible before venturing from town. For once, he had no desire to draw attention to himself.

He drove well within the speed limit, for he'd recently learned that a number of Highway Safety patrolmen had returned within the month from an insidious brainwashing at the FBI's training academy at Quantico, Virginia, and that these particular troopers could not be joshed out of a traffic ticket. Attempting to slip them a twenty to help with their household expenses was said to be cause for a one-way ride to Jackson in the caged back of a cruiser. Furthermore, it had been learned that these officers were gathering intelligence on the White Knights and passing it on to their communistic puppeteers up north.

Townley slowed for the Coca-Cola carton leaning against the base of a dogwood tree—a signal instantly recognizable to any klansman. Next, the federal bastards would be on to this secret as well. It was vital today he impress upon the brotherhood that informers would be dealt with in most severe fashion, that the capital sentence called for in the Prescript, or constitution, was not an idle boast.

He turned onto the dirt road, then stopped in a cloud of dust raised by his own tires. The recent rain, like most summer downpours in this part of the country, had been spotty, drenching town but skipping over this neck of the woods. Grumbling, he got out and put up the convertible top.

Back behind the wheel, he wiped his gator-skin boots with his handkerchief, which he tossed into the brush before rolling up the windows and continuing on toward the small hill obscured by the trees.

Atop it, Lester Cowens, Floyd Swilley, and Curtis Foy were standing guard on the steps of the antebellum clapboard Methodist church. They were crading rifles in their arms, and a smiling Townley could almost imagine them in Confederate gray. These were good men at heart, full of cheer and courage in the midst of this present adversity, men worthy of the recent rebirth of the Klan after decades of decline.

But then he frowned, for he wanted to show that he hadn't liked the suddenness of this summons. The FBI was tearing southwest Mississippi apart for some trace of the White Knights, and Townley had insisted to the brotherhood that a gathering of any sort was to be convened only under the direst of circumstances.

"This better be damn important," he said to the three men, slamming the car door.

Not one of them spoke up. And they glanced at one another as if puzzled.

Sensing that something was wrong, Townley hurried into the church. Cowens and Foy followed him inside while Swilley remained on watch outside.

Occupying the front pew were Ray Stuckey, Clint Pell, and the Cooke brothers, Earl and Wesley. All looked expectantly at Townley.

"Who the devil called this meeting?" he demanded.

"Why, you did, Clay," Stuckey said slowly and distinctly as if he might be talking to an amnesiac.

"Of this group? What the hell do you think, man, I'm out of my fucking mind?"

Lester Cowens sank down into the rear pew. "Oh shit . . . no, no, no . . ." Then, on a sudden thought, he threw himself to his feet and hollered out the door: "Swilley, you see anybody out there?"

"Settle down," Pell said, although the hand holding his cigarette was shaking a little. "Everybody just keep hold of hisself and settle down."

"Is this some bullshit setup?" Cowens went on, waving his .30-caliber carbine. "Clay, you absolutely sure you didn't call this, now? My wife gave me the message. She wrote it down. She said you wanted me to pass on the message to Ray and Clint right away at the courthouse—"

"Lester, will you shut up for one goddamn minute?" Townley whistled for Swilley's attention: "Speak to us, Floyd. You see or hear anything?"

"Not a thing, Clay," the big man answered, backing inside through the propped-open front door, but keeping his eyes and his rifle trained on the woods. Want me to take a wander through the trees?"

"No. We're all pulling out of here *now*. But one question first—where's Lyle?"

"Tilman left this morning for Jackson," Stuckey answered. "Some mayor's convention or something."

"Confirm that, Ray. I hope to Jesus Christ he

was tellir.g the truth. Now, let's get. But not in a mess. Earl and Wesley, you boys drive away first. Hit your horn twice if everything looks okay on the highway. I'll leave second."

Ward remained in the Polara while Anderson got out and strolled inside the gas station office. He smiled around the small room. In the corner on a stool sat an old man, his receding lower jaw and sunken cheeks grizzled by a week's growth. Leaning against the wall, his left leg cocked under him, a youth in an oil-stained baseball cap was fiddling with his spool key ring. Presiding over this sullen-looking group was Lester Cowens, who ignored Anderson's friendly nod.

"Howdy, Lester," the agent said. "You ready?"

"Ready for what?"

"Why, your ride. I know you said five sharp. But we got tied up."

Cowens grinned, but couldn't hide his growing bewilderment. "You're cracked."

"Don't you always go to the social club after work?"

"Sure, but—"

Anderson had walked out. Unseen by anyone in the office, he winked at Ward as if to say that Cowens had swallowed the bait.

"What the hell you trying to pull, Hoover boy?" Cowens asked, coming outside. Then he saw Ward. "Oh you," he said, contemptuously. "Y'all here to clean my clock?"

Ward smiled widely for the benefit of the old man and the youth, who were now pressed up against the inside of the dirty office window. "I apologize for my behavior that night, Lester. I was way out of line."

"You sure was."

"Get in," Anderson said.

"In where?"

"The car, for Lord's sake."

"Your car?"

"Yes, our car."

Cowens stared first at one agent and then the other with large, unblinking eyes. Anderson had seen far more intelligent gazes in the dairy herd Ward and he had passed on their return from scoping out the Methodist church. In the same fluid motion of opening the door for Cowens, he brushed up against the man and—shielding his ruse from office view with his torso—put a twistlock on Lester's right wrist.

Cowens gasped from the stab of pain, but Anderson said, "Cry out, and I'll break it." Just to assure him that he was serious, the agent gave him another little wrenching jolt, which sent Cowens to his toes as lightly as a ballerina. "Do we got an understanding?"

"Yeah," Cowens hissed, "stop it, please. You're breaking it."

"Not even close, friend. You got two more levels of pain to feel before she snaps on you. Wave with a smile to your buddies and get inside the car."

Cowens did so, sliding across the seat and rubbing his chafed wrist as soon as Anderson released it.

Ward immediately drove out of the station lot and toward Main Street.

"What call y'all got to do this?" Cowens shouted, but Anderson could tell by the man's unclenched hands that the unexpectedly engrossing pain of the twistlock had stolen the fight out of him. Anderson was glad: Cowens looked like he could hunt bear with a hickory switch.

"What gives Mr. Ward and me the right, Lester? The fact that you went along for the ride that night the three kids were murdered."

A mask fell over Cowens's face. "I ain't got nothing to say."

"You make this a whole lot easier on yourself and your family if you go on the record right now," Anderson said.

"You're barking up the wrong tree."

"Lester, you should know something," Ward said from the front seat—he was slowly driving past the courthouse. "We already have all seven of you cold. One of your compatriots saw the light."

"What's that supposed to mean?"

"He talked," Anderson said. "Hell, he wore out our recorder's little machine he talked so much."

"You're lying."

Anderson exhaled. "This is your last chance to get aboard, Lester. I'm telling you, friend, the federal leniency train is pulling out of the station, and in about another two seconds you're gonna find yourself standing on the platform holding nothing but your cock. We know you drove the second vehicle. It was your blue Ford pickup."

Cowens was now occupying his half of the rear seat as if it were an electric chair. He started to speak, hesitated, then pressed his thin lips together. For the first time he seemed to realize that the eyes of the entire town were fixed on the black Dodge Polara—and him in the back of it.

"And your buddy says you . . ." Anderson tapped Ward on the shoulder. "Kindly refresh my memory, Mr. Ward, on how the homicide transpired."

"Our informant says Lester Cowens dragged

the Negro victim from the car by the hair, kicked him twice in the face, and then shot him."

"That's a goddamn lie."

Anderson chuckled. "Oh, it's true as scripture, Lester. You got some more there, Mr. Ward?"

"Yes. Lester Cowens then said, 'They only left me a nigger, but at least I shot me a nigger.'"

"I didn't kill him!" he blurted. "I only shot him in the ass."

Anderson let the words hang in the air for a long moment so Cowens could realize that he'd just crossed a line he could never shrink behind again. Then the agent said, "Oh, I believe that's a real possibility, Lester, that the Negro kid was already dead when you put a slug in him. But that's a fine point, and you know how fine points can stack up against a fella in a court of law. Particularly a federal court. But anyways, your buddy tells it different. He swears you killed the kid, so it's his word against yours. You have a pleasant toddy now, Lester."

Ward had stopped in front of the social club.

As if in a trance, Cowens got out of the Dodge and, without looking back, shambled inside the Quonset hut.

"You want to grab a bite with me, Al?" Anderson asked, hoping that his voice didn't sound unnatural. On the drive back down Main Street to the theater, he had spotted Clinton Pell's patrol car parked in front of the barbershop.

As anticipated, Ward said, "No, thanks, you go ahead. I'd like to make sure everything is set for tonight." Then he added: "To make sure all the men know their limitations during this caper."

For once Anderson didn't argue with Ward. "See you in a couple, then."

He crossed the street, casually almost, but then bore down on the barber's pole as if it were a beacon. His hands became fists, and his eyes began moistening as his rage welled inside him. He could hear his pulse roaring in his ears—the swishing of a vengeance that would not be denied. These were unfamiliar sensations; he had never even felt them during the war, and the phrase—"A shot fired in anger"—had always been something of joke to him. He had never fired a shot in anger, even after his best friend in the platoon had been killed. He, like the others, had done all his shooting in a vortex of fear, the dread of the sudden death that seemed inevitable the longer a man was on the line, and that utter helplessness in the face of horrific modern weapons like Tiger tanks and 88mm. shells.

But this evening, twenty years and five thousand miles from the Ardennes, he knew that he was finally going to loose a shot in anger.

Pell and the barber were alone in the shop, the deputy lathered all the way up to his closed eyes.

Without a word Anderson relieved the barber of his straight razor and jerked his thumb for the man to leave. That he did so without protesting gave Anderson some indication of what his own face looked like.

"What's the wait, Bill?" Clinton Pell mumbled sleepily.

"Sorry, it's a long time since I did this." And then he nicked the deputy, drawing a trickle of blood that seemed vivid against the snowy shaving cream.

Pell's eyes snapped open, although the rest of his face remained absolutely still.

Anderson started shaving him. "I got a question for you, Clint. You don't mind if I call you Clint, do you, now? I feel like I know you so well. See, the way we got it, on the night following the murders when y'all watched as the bulldozer buried the kids, you made a short speech. Something like 'Mississippi can be proud of us. We've struck a blow for the white man.' Am I pretty close to chapter and verse, Clint?"

Anderson glanced down: Pell's hands were whitely clutching he armrests.

"It had to be you who said it, Clint. Clayton Townley and Ray Stuckey are too smart to hang around a murder burial and make Fourth of July orations. And you're too boneheaded to ever realize somebody would remember what you said."

Again Anderson nicked him. "Oops. This is damn tricky, ain't it, though? Barber makes it look so easy. Just like anything else, I suppose. A killing, for instance. A hitman makes it look simple. But it really isn't. Killing is a business lousy with all kinds of pitfalls. A regular mine field, killing." Then he pressed the razor against Pell's carotid artery, a dim voice reminding him that he was within a pound of pressure of slitting it open. "Did you make a speech the night you thumped your wife, Clint? Did you strike a blow for the white man that night?"

Then the voice inside Anderson's head became even dimmer. The razor began trembling wildly in his grasp.

The barber got no more than "Pell and your fella" out of his mouth than Ward began sprinting down the street. He was half sick with the thought that he might have to shoot one of his own, that he might have to kill Rupert Anderson in order to save Clinton Pell.

Yet when he grasped the doorjamb and swung inside the barbershop, Anderson was tossing a straight razor into the sink and the deputy was slumping unhurt—but for a few neck scratches—in the chair.

The brows of both men were glistening with sweat.

Anderson nodded in Ward's direction, then said hoarsely to Pell, "Make no mistake. I'd gladly cut your head clean off and then go to the joint grinning from ear to ear. That's how I feel about it, *Clint*."

Then he walked out, passing Ward without meeting his eyes.

The silence awaiting Lester Cowens inside the Quonset hut had quickly gotten on his nerves. He started to explain to Frank Bailey and Earl Cooke, the only men who hadn't glared at him when he attempted to sit at their table, how the two FBI men had kidnapped him in broad daylight and forced him to go with them to—

"Your own goddamn social club, Lester?" Frank Bailey had interrupted at that point. The bald suspicion in his longtime friend's voice had triggered Cowens's own anger, and he had called both him and Earl son of bitches, caustically thanking them for their hospitality and storming out of the place.

Home now, he was trying to settle down with a bourbon and milk at the kitchen table and figure things out.

But Marliss kept passing back and forth in front of him for no reason at all other than to distract him and make him pay her and Lester Junior some mind. The supper dishes had been dried and shelved an hour ago.

"That goddamn baby grafted to your hip or something?" he snapped at her.

She slowly turned her broad, freckled face at him. "He ain't no 'goddamn' baby, Lester James. He's your son. And he cries when I put him down. You want me to set him on down so he can cry and you can bitch about that too?"

No, he didn't want to bitch about that.

In truth, he wanted to talk about the enormous trouble he sensed coming his way, but was afraid that if he unburdened himself to Marliss, she would blame him for being stupid and hotheaded. Her daddy had always said that the Cowens boys were "stupid as stumps and hotheaded as rhubarb," and he wasn't about to confirm something the old bastard had said, even if he was dead and buried fifteen years now. Even from the grave, that man seemed to go on criticizing him.

He took another gulp of milk and bourbon, hoping the whiskey would calm his jangled nerves and the milk would soothe his burning gut. On a far better day than this one, Frank Bailey had recommended the drink to him for when his guts were afire but he still needed liquor, bad.

Then a blast outside gave him a fright that shook the glass right out of his hand.

It had been a shotgun report.

The baby started wailing, but Cowens had the presence of mind to tell Marliss: "Get down, woman! Crawl down to the cellar!"

As she scampered along the hallway toward the

cellar door with Lester Junior under her hammy arm, Cowens doused every light in the place from the breaker box, then duck-walked toward the parlor of the old farmhouse. The bay windows there provided the best view of the milo field between the house and the county road a half mile to the west.

His carbine was still in his Ford pickup. He damned himself for not thinking to bring it inside. His twelve-gauge was upstairs, but he'd been meaning to buy some shells after he'd used up his supply rabbit hunting.

He crossed the darkened parlor on his belly. Parting the curtains no more than an inch, he peered outside—and the indigo evening erupted into flames which spread up into the shape of a cross.

"Shit!" He rolled over and over to the front door and cracked it. "Boys! What's this about now?" he hollered, vaguely ashamed that his voice sounded so frightened. "You must be assuming something that just ain't! Talk to me, dammit!"

He was answered with a prolonged crump-crump-crump of shotgun fire. He didn't hear any pellets strike the pine-board side of the old house, but he decided to take no chances. Rising no higher than a crouch, he bolted back to the kitchen and out the screen door, almost taking it with him.

He fully expected to be shot on his way across the yard to his pickup, but this risk seemed better than being trapped inside the house. He knew all too well what Molotov cocktails could do to a structure that had been slowly drying out for a century or more.

He always left the key in the ignition, and thankfully it was still there. This made him feel better, superior almost to these yokels. He would have removed it, even disabled the old truck had he been in their shoes.

Deciding not to use his headlamps, he rounded the barn and joined the dirt track that connected his place to the county road. By the light of the burning cross behind him, he saw that another pickup, a one-ton GMC by the cut of it, had fallen in behind him, also running without lights. And then ahead, nearly as far as the county road, two pinpricks of yellowish light could be seen flickering this way through the milo—yet another vehicle, this one blocking his most likely avenue of escape.

Turning the wheel hard, he began following the old logging road his daddy had bladed forty years before to harvest the last stand of red maple in the entire county. It was really no more than two weathered ruts running across a tall grass prairie that eventually descended westward into swampland, but long before he came to any standing water Cowens discovered that the cloudburst this week had freshened the mud. His worn tires were already slipping and sloshing when a sudden jolt from behind drove his forehead against the inside of the windshield.

"Christ!"

He was sure when his dazed vision returned to him that he would see both blood and broken glass, but there was neither.

"Damn y'all to hell!"

He braced himself for the next ramming.

And it came so forcefully his front tires jumped the ruts and the Ford slewed out into the mud. The heavier GMC slammed against it one last time, but the half-ton Ford was going nowhere soon. It was mired up to the running boards.

Cowens thought of his carbine behind the seat, but then realized that he could never live here again if he resorted to gunplay.

His only hope lay in escape.

He could hear the GMC's engine rumbling behind him as he flew out of the cab and slogged up toward the wooded ridge that now separated him from his house. And he was gazing over his shoulder at the silhouette of the one-ton when he collided with a man who, responding quicker than Cowens, shoved him aside.

He stumbled down into the dewy grass, but hurriedly flopped over on his back to fend off any coming blows.

The man looming over him was wearing a flour sack hood.

"Please," Cowens begged, no longer concerned that his voice sounded scared, "I didn't say nothing. I swear to the Lord Savior it's a setup!"

A boot glanced off his forearm. "Please, hoss! Talk to me now!"

But the man remained silent. Beyond him Cowens could dimly see two others in hoods tramping up the slope. As they got nearer, he realized that one of them was carrying a coil of rope.

"No!" He had begun to blubber. "I didn't say nothing, I tell you!"

A fist found his face again and again, but he didn't resist the numbing blows. He felt heavy with helplessness, even sleepy in an odd sort of way. He didn't think he could run now. Besides, it didn't seem like the thing to do. Yet he continued to cry and beg for the life he somehow sensed he had already lost.

His hands were tethered behind his back. "Please, boys, you got to believe me!"

Again, nothing but silence from them.

"Take me to Clay, then. Let Townley decide. He'll tell you I'm innocent!"

One of them chuckled, but Cowens couldn't tell by the brief laugh which of his Klan brothers had issued it. He didn't believe they were close by any tree, but when he glanced skyward he was shocked to see a dead limb sprawling massively up into the evening stars.

The noose was dropped around his neck, then snugged tight, and he began sobbing without words. Somebody kicked him in back, but he figured it was just out of meanness and not intended to make him stop crying. They probably enjoyed his crying. He fell over on his side. But as he did he thought he saw a glimmer of headlamps.

He raised his head: a dark-colored Dodge sedan had pulled in behind the GMC. He knew at once that it was an FBI car, and when he heard footfalls retreating behind him, the kluckers racing for concealment on top of the ridge, he rejoiced that it was the FBI.

As Anderson and he started up the muddy incline toward Lester Cowens, Ward whispered, "You are to do exactly as I order, Mr. Anderson. Anything *but* will result in disciplinary action." He had not yet forgotten the confrontation in the barbershop only four hours ago.

"You know," Anderson said quietly, his first complete sentence since then, "never let up when you got the chance to do in somebody you hate. You may think at the time you might later regret it. But you won't. It's pulling back you'll regret." However, his voice turned gentle as he approached a whimpering Cowens: "Christ, but you look a mess, Lester. You're damn lucky we been watching your ass."

Ward removed the noose. "If you go on the record, Cowens, we'll protect you. If not, they're going to kill you anyway. We're all you have left." He and Anderson helped him to his feet. "This is my last offer."

Snuffling, Cowens mumbled something Ward finally realized to be a yes.

"You're a smart man, Lester," Anderson said, peering at three men running across the top of ridge, backlit by the rising moon.

Ward too watched as agents Brodsky, Nash, and Macmillan—still in their flour sack hoods—circled around so they could remove the GMC pickup as soon as Cowens was driven away to be interrogated.

Epilogue

And then one morning in Jackson, for most intents and purposes, it was finished.

The eight defendants stood stiffly in their church suits, hands clasped before them, and the federal judge ended two months of legal bickering by passing out the sentences as unceremoniously as if he were assigning some high school gym students their lockers for the coming term.

With two years to be served in a minimum-security detention center in Missouri, Lester Cowens's term was at the low end of the range, thanks to his early cooperation. The seven others were bound for the federal penitentiary at Marion, Illinois. At the middle of the pack, bartender Frank Bailey would be locked up for seven years, which appeared to please them only when they heard that Clinton Pell would be at Marion more than twice as long as they would—fifteen years.

The former deputy sheriff showed no emotion as the federal marshal beckoned him to lead the file of seven others through the side door of the courtroom that would begin their incarceration.

Peering out the tall window at the maple whose

foliage had gradually gone from pale green to scarlet over these weeks, Ward asked himself how he felt.

Certainly not ebullient.

Perhaps his subdued mood had something to do with the fact that two of the suspects in the events of that June night were not present.

In late August, when the first grand-jury indictments were handed down and his name appeared on one of them, Mayor Lyle Tilman had gotten moderately drunk on his most expensive bottle of gin, then descended the wooden steps into his cellar, where he hanged himself with a spare fan belt for his Cadillac.

And then there was Clayton Townley.

The grand wizard had withdrawn to his hometown of Tupelo, where, under the pressure of constant FBI surveillance, he had become a recluse, a shadow behind the chemise curtains of his sprawling ranch-style house. His indictment was imminent, although the U.S. attorney had wanted it held off until as much evidence as possible could be gathered against him. His conviction would be the toughest of all to win, but Ward trusted that Townley would wind up serving time in the warm camaraderie of his fellow White Knights.

He had half expected Anderson to ride along with him this morning for the sentencing. Other than for his own day of testimony on the stand, the agent had been excluded from the proceedings as a witness. Only Ward, as the principal investigator, had been present for it all. But now that it was coming to a close, the case seemed to be of little interest to Anderson, an annoying memory, ancient history.

Ward pulled back his sleeve and checked his wristwatch: ten-thirty.

He could have the theater completely closed down by two. Anderson and he could be on the road by three. The sale of the motel, which the Bureau had purchased to avoid the eviction of its agents early in the investigation, would have to be turned over to the Jackson office; property—like everything else—did not move quickly in southwest Mississippi.

He rose.

Outside, the bright autumn morning lifted his spirits a bit. "You did it, Boss," he said out loud, beginning to smile. "The son of bitches didn't get away with it."

"I may be a minute or two, Al," Anderson said, getting out of the Dodge in front of the Pell house.

"Take your time."

He started toward the veranda, frowning at the screens that had been slashed and the windows shattered by rocks. The lawn was completely dead for lack of watering; there was also a big scorched spot in it where the cross had stood.

She met him at the screen door. Her facial bruises had faded to a pale yellow, but her left arm was still in a sling.

"Hi," he said.

"Hi." She smiled, which made him feel better about dropping by. He had written a letter, but it had wound up in the trash basket of his motel room.

"I missed you at the hospital this morning. They said you'd come home."

"What's left of it." She opened the screen door

for him to come inside, then offered Ward a shy wave. He nodded back at her.

Shards of window glass were strewn over the living room furniture and carpet. "Damn."

"Yeah . . ." She smiled again, but it was more fragile than the one the moment before. "Damn."

"What will you do?"

"I don't know."

"Where will you go?" he asked, thinking his question only reasonable under the circumstances.

But she surprised him. "Oh, I'm not going anywhere. I'm staying. This is my home." A dustpan lay in the middle of the floor. Kneeling, she began collecting the glass splinters with her free hand. He started to help her, but she stopped him with a brief frown. "If I wanted to leave, I would have done it a long time ago, believe me, Mr. Anderson. Things will work out." When his expression turned skeptical, she added, "There's enough good people around here to know what I did was right. Especially after what came out in the trial. And there's enough ladies who like the way I fix their hair. Besides, it's fall. I love this sad old town in fall." She avoided his eyes as she came to her feet. "And what will you do?"

"Back to Memphis for the time being. There's some talk my old boss in St. Louis wants me working for him again. But I'll take about any field office where my accent don't stick out like a sore thumb." He fell silent, looking at her. "Mr. Ward out there has got himself a dandy promotion," he went on, saying anything to delay the moment that was swiftly approaching. "He's to clear out his desk in Memphis, then fly to Albany."

"New York?"

"Yes, I don't think he'd get on too well in Georgia. But, regardless, he's gonna take over Albany as special agent-in-charge."

"Sounds like quite a job for a man of his years."

"It is. But he'll do fine. He'll go far."

"And you, Mr. Anderson? How far will you go?"

"Oh, I'm long done with trying to squeeze myself into places I don't fit. Like you, I know where I belong." Then there was nothing more to be said, and he realized the moment had arrived. He held out his hand, and she slid hers into his. " 'Bye, Mrs. Pell."

" 'Bye, Mr. Anderson."

"It's been real nice knowing you."

As her eyes clouded, he turned and let himself out.

He was almost to the Dodge when she called to him from the veranda: "Mr. Anderson?"

"Yes, Mrs. Pell?"

"Will you send me a postcard now and then?"

"You can count on it."

"But you don't know my first name."

Climbing into the car, he chuckled softly before calling back to her, "Of course I know your first name. What kind of cop do you think I am?" Then he said to Ward, "Drive away, Boss, before I change my goddamn mind and run for sheriff down here. And don't be too surprised if I buy a half gallon and get flat ruint tonight."

"I just might join you, Rupert."

"Then I'm holding you to your word." Anderson looked back one last time, and it made him feel inordinately pleased to see that she was still standing on the veranda, waving.